T0328483

FINDING A WAY HOME

*

Stories

Tendai Rinos Mwanaka

Mwanaka Media and Publishing Pvt Ltd,
Chitungwiza Zimbabwe

*

Creativity, Wisdom and Beauty

Publisher: *Mmap*

Mwanaka Media and Publishing Pvt Ltd

24 Svosve Road, Zengeza 1

Chitungwiza Zimbabwe

mwanaka@yahoo.com

mwanaka13@gmail.com

https://www.mmapublishing.org

www.africanbookscollective.com/publishers/mwanaka-media-and-publishing

https://facebook.com/MwanakaMediaAndPublishing/

Distributed in and outside N. America by African Books Collective

orders@africanbookscollective.com

www.africanbookscollective.com

ISBN: 978-1-77931-487-1

EAN: 9781779314871

ii

TABLE OF CONTENTS

PROLOGUE

When we are born we leave our first real homes, our mother's wombs. We try to create home in that place we are in, usually in our early childhood homes, and these become our real homes, as long as we are still closer to where we came from, that is, near our parents. As we grow older, the more subtracted we are from where we came, the more we move away from home. It reminds me of Charles Beinstein, 1979 reading his poem, *In a restless world like this is*, at the Kyler Writers Centre, Philadelphia, saying, "As far as you go in one direction, all the further you have to go on, before the way back has become totally indivisible". The more we move far away from our earlier homes, the more we might have to go, maybe a lifetime of it for us, to cut that connection we had with that earlier childhood home. We might really spend our entire lives travelling, and maybe the beauty is on the travel itself. In making the way back totally indivisible to this earlier home, we have to create new homes for ourselves. Some people do not have the wherewithal to move away from these earlier homes, some do not have the power, some are unwilling, thus they stay closer to that earlier home, some even die before they have moved much, thus returning to their home (originating or ending). In the memoir story, *When he was still closer home*, I tried to bring this idea out.

iv

This home is a place in ourselves where we are happy with ourselves, where we find peace with ourselves, where we are satisfied, fulfilled. The important theme coursing through all the stories in the novel, *Finding a way home*, is that we have to make the journey to find our homes, we have to find the path, and start walking in that path. The story that the whole collection borrows its title from, *Finding a way home*, is whereby four men are sent to a faraway kingdom to answer to a plea of help from a king in that far away kingdom, in Africa, in the earlier ages. The four start this journey with so much enthusiasm, but they discover this journey, this travel was merciless, but they also find their way to their homes, to their true worth. Home is where each of the four traveler's heart is and their heart is where their truth is. Each of the four sends his head to where they end up. In each, every time, home is a sanctuary, so it is to each of the characters in the entire book. Each character, some early and some late, establishes where their 'home' is, and mapped the maze that life builds for each around it. Home will be at core, its source. Like a salmon can find its way miles upstream, back to its beginnings, you can find your way back home should you need to.

The stories in *Finding a way home*, tackle many of the experiences of a Zimbabwean people, but mostly life in the last decade or so: i.e. life during the fight for democracy in Zimbabwe. It also tackles rape and sexual abuse issues, an insight into diseases that are not usually talked about well in Africa, yet they are devastating the continent just like AIDS, Malaria, TB; diseases like bipolar, hypertension, cancer. It tackles failure of religious and spiritual beliefs. It delves into early adult coming-of-age stories, love stories in a world in the shadow of the AIDS pandemic, our dire need as humans to want to connect our lives with someone else, especially now in the 21st century and how mostly it is ending in break-ups of relationships and disillusionment. "It is worth realizing that 'home' for you is not necessarily 'home' for your partner or others in your immediate family. You can all be travelling, simultaneously, to different places," I noted in the essay, *Home*. In these love stories, I also explore the psychological, spiritual and emotional wreck one can be, when dealing with a failed relationship.

My stories are free of most of the conventions of storytelling. Some stories are like notes, of different people connected to this idea of *Finding a way home*, talking... Telling their own stories, in their own way, I don't always use the conventional modes of storytelling. In this attempt, I also explore storytelling techniques; in having the characters in the stories stamp their own emotions on the page. It is very experimental, challenging and incisive, the stories have the ability to look a subject straight in eyes, without flinching. It is sometimes a fractured narrative with phrases disappearing off the edges. But I also had to balance between the exhibit of preciseness use of language and a deeper observation of human behaviour at close range through observing it all like a camera.

There are stories about animals. I have the telling of two stories into one coherent story, the mixing of many other genres (diary, essays, dreams, poetry, memoirs, philosophical discourse, travelogue, paint with words etc...) with the storytelling genre. I try to connect these stories by telling them in part stories that will come in on different parts of the book, thus connecting the book into one story.

Just because the stories comes from these different confluences, so it pervades time, space, and place. There are stories set in the Zimbabwean country side, stories of Zimbabwean cities, especially Chitungwiza-Harare, where I have stayed most of the last 20 years, and they are stories I started writing over 20 years ago, for instance, *And These Were Their Reasons,* and stories from South Africa where I lived as an expatriate for two and half years, stories from earlier times Africa, or the World. It also sprawls across different cultural systems, beliefs, and lives, but it still is fundamentally about, *Finding a way home.*

Therefore, the biggest import of this collection is about finding your way to your home; that we have to search very deeply within ourselves for the right path to our home, and start with the baby steps, walking in this road. When we are in our rightful path we are so confident because we know it would eventually lead us home, but the way is fraught with difficulties, and it's these difficulties I also lighted on in this collection.

Dreams, Paintings, Light

The skinned
Haloed light
Hello you *light!*
The *light* that sweeps and whispers
Of the birthing room
At Mount Mellery Mission Hospital, missing it he remembers it, when his mother was giving birth to a sister: Katarina. Giving his sister birth/giving birth to his sister, is the act of giving, giving, giving...

It's this light; it's this smell...*a light that smells.* He was born there; he remembers his birth in misremembering it. The memory of which is like a dream of the backbone in which the backbone rapes its own memory. Not rape but, abuse its memory!

He doesn't like it much, not his birth. He was happy to leave the room. He knew a *birthing room* is where death and life fights. It's the fighting that he is always having in his *dreams,* fighting for his life, his sanity.
He wins the fights by *painting light,*
Painting light; light that is hardly like *light,* it sustains, it illuminates but it exacts nothing from anyone.

He has been sleepwalking. He has been doing that every night. Some nights, he would write, some nights he would sing, some nights he would take his camera and take pictures, some nights he would *paint*, draw figures, sketches on his canvass, inside him. He knows he would be doing all these, when he sleepwalks away from his *fighting dreams*, but he faintly remembers doing: music, visual art, photography. It is nights when he writes and *paints* that he remembers. He finds the manuscripts (canvasses) on his bed, sometimes.

Sometimes they would stay long on his brain, to reproduce them; sometimes he has to use his imagination to reproduce them, the *light* in his imaginations straining and shabby.
He has started *painting*, lately.
He borrowed the *paint* brush from his brother-in-law, to *paint* his house. But he hasn't been able to do that, yet,
He doesn't want to!

During the days, he looks at the brushes and, he knows it's something he wouldn't be doing very soon, *painting* the house. It's his code in the desert he has created, inside himself. He is afraid if he were to *paint* the house, the *painting dreams* would go, and he wouldn't know how to deal with the loss,
Bereft feelings,
The fights,
He has to keep away from it.
It's at night when he uses these brushes.

And this night he started to want to *paint* in his *dreams. Painting* is when he finds calm, in his sleep. If he doesn't do one of the art things above, he has to fight the whole night, fighting things he doesn't understand. There are all sorts of battles, sometimes he

2

has to travel, to walk. They are *river dreams*, rivers he will be trying to cross, monsters stopping him.

He had been *dreaming* such a *dream,*

Or is it *re-dreaming* such a *dream?*

He knew he had had that *dream* before.

He was walking off to somewhere, with a girl, he had been dating, Cynthia. She loves him, she tells him she does, and he sees she tries, but his heart is not in it.

Can one try to love?

Engineering love, or even re-engineering love?

He doesn't know!

How much this woman wanted meaning, but inside him layer upon layer of him was floating.

He has stopped seeing her, it's two times now. When he had this *dream*, he had stopped for the second time.

He would stop again, he knows, before he finds her, before he loses himself in her *light* and shades.

Maybe he is scared of committing to someone, to die into someone. Is that not what love is, dying, to revolve (rapture) between sky and earth? *Boom bang pwaa, pfuchuuu…*

She is coming, he doesn't know from where, and she is going back to her place. Sometimes, it's like in Chitungwiza where he stays, sometimes it looks like in Johannesburg, where he has stayed. He is talking to her, then she starts moving faster, trying to lose him, but he follows her. They arrive at the place she stays, it's a brothel. She runs into the insides, leaving him outside. At that moment, its deep gutted inside him, how much he wanted her to teach him how to evolve from quivering fins to bursting stars! But, the Guard refuses him entry inside…but someone, a block away, beckons him over. She tells him, the girl is a hooker girl. She shows him a path to use, into this room she has disappeared into. He follows her, he enters the building, and then he realises its empty in the insides!

No house, no rooms, nothing, not her!

There is nothing inside but an articulate silence that explains everything,

She has disappeared.

He leaves for home, there is a dam he skirts on his way. There are stepping stones, and he doesn't fall into the waters…he keeps going home. He starts fighting things, some with the intent to kill him, some to waylay him from his path home.

He stays focused…he keeps walking…but he doesn't reach home.

And then, he is returning back.

He doesn't know why he is returning. He didn't find the home, and in his returning, there is something that is still calling him, to go home, but he can't seem to. The way home, there is now this huge river. When he looks at it, he knows he can't cross it. The monsters are inside…so he keeps going, not home.

He is so dead, his feelings are.

He thinks the only way to do is to back flip onto the way home.

He is troubled!

So, he takes the bigger brush…

He starts *painting* the dawn, in the sky he is seeing. There are cracks in the dawn….where there was *light, grey light* comes and swings hard to the left, and they are rain clouds foaming that knits a nest of air and space. And the air crosses clouds in hot nets increasing the local air's tenor uprightness. He has *painted* these rain clouds before. After quiet a long time, in which he is *painting and painting* the sky…there is an opening in the greying skies, or is it considerably less grey. And then, the sky finds its tongue and stutters a few syllables of spring, *lightning light*. The scene has changed abruptly, dramatically, although nothing in his insides has changed.

The dawn is falling away…

It's getting dark on the western sky, though the east…there is the beginning of the coming sun, the *sun's light*. The wind has died down a little and the *light* is more intense in the east, and less and less intense in the west. High up those eastern horizons, the horizon blushes for him, and it's the extraordinary voluptuousness that pervades high places that astonishes him. He is in the middle of such a sky!

The rows of columns of clouds to the west seem to float with their *light capitals*, and their invisible foundations, and he expected, at any moment, to see their delicate shafts breaking up in their moving waves, like reflections in water.

He is in the middle of such a play of *light*.
His soul is flooded with too much *light*.

5

In the western skies *creviced light* floods, near him into damned places in his insides. And these damned places inside him are haloed out arenas, black holes, *lassoed in light*. In the east *new light* flooding in, is miraculous energy, *light diving* in like an eagle, such accuracy and surprise mesmerises him.

It's a sun-kissed benediction.

But, he doesn't feel it's enough for him. The river still calls him-Home calls him. It's like he almost has epiphany, a date with it!

Painting the sky doesn't stop him from wanting to go home…

So, he takes the smaller brush, rubbish brush, *painter's brush*, round brush, brittle unbroken brush, a maker's brush, brushing… The western sky becomes completely hidden by a fast moving cloud of *dark light*, whispering dampness, and the wind is now exhilarating. He tries to *paint* his own portrait, using flaming hues of red passion for his favourite T-shirt, smooth beach water blue for his well-worn shorts, soul brother brown for his rafters, his skin, and double electric green blended around his portrait, together creating this person.

Is that my head…it looks too big!

His frame is shooting *a bold ray of light* cascading beauty and wisdom. But, still the *light of his dreaming* is not unfurled.

He decides to go home.

He starts moving again, *into his dream…*

He has his two brushes. He knows he could *paint* when it becomes too much for him. There are some people he identifies, because they are friendly, but doesn't know their names.

It's now an extension of *the first dream…*

6

He has to cross the river. Its muddy, fully flooded. A toe in the water would take him downwards, or into the world of the monsters. He gets to the river's edges, eventually, after a long walk. The monster unfurls water as it dives for him. It's a monster shark thing with teeth flung out to gulp him. He avoids its huge blow by a whisker..., as he runs off the river. It splatters heavily, into flesh and blood, blooding the rocky road, just behind him. He doesn't stop to check, he runs off. He knows this one is dead. But, he also knows another is still alive in the water. Suddenly, he reaches some building, and finds shelter there. He tells these people he identifies but do not know their names; that the other monster is on its way. They say they would destroy it. He doesn't wait to see, how. He keeps running, but he is seeing what's happening,
With his behind eyes!
They have created a huge wall.
In his *dream*, he is running but he is seeing the scene.

He stops his mind from running with his body by *painting* again. A *light* in his canvass is like one in which everyone, all those people who are fighting the monster for him are from another year, not old, not young, but who they were... he doesn't know? He tries, and fails, to make *the play of light* defines these people.

Only that they are now different, enlivened in their task; bright, beautifully bright, *in yellowed light*.
It's like the *light* is showing him how one person maybe ensouled through the continued experience of others.

7

Bathed in a light, unreal air, into new clarities...
There is a moon to the south!

The moon licks him with its *shinning mould of lighting speed*. He says, to himself; One day he would be the moon, and stand at someone's window, *shedding light*. He looks at the scene again.
All he sees is the way the *moon's light* reaches and holds the scene together, and everything is now displayed structure, splay structure, lyrical leisure and strange comeuppance.
And then, the monster thing hits the walls, and splatters into blood. Everyone shouts in joy,
It is dead!

Whilst the bloated sky he had painted, sky-burst its grey wetness into the streets, RAIN, it doesn't matter where; it descends and, it follows the curve of the earth. He loves rain
In his soul, he sees himself crossing the river.
He laughs at the moon so hard that it might give up on its stars. Suddenly everything is alright for him, *in his dreams*. He is on his bed, sleeping.

When he wakes up...

He will wake up from this night, lucid and alive, remembering it all! He knows he has created a masterpiece, in his head.
This is one canvas he will keep.

MOCK FUNERAL

"You have what is known as bipolar disorder 1..., simply, in layman terms, you have maniac mood swings...one moment you might be contemplating killing yourself, and another moment you are ok, one moment you want to laugh, another you are sad, one moment you are angry and another you are happy..."

"What causes this condition, doctor?"

"It is partly inherited, partly caused by the environment you inhabit, and partly caused by neurological malfunctions. It occurs in a sizable part of the population, but usually with some minor mood shifts."

"How can I minimize it, doctor; it is affecting my relationship with my fiancé?"

John couldn't face having to keep lying to his fiancé, why sometimes when she wants to see him, he was somewhere else...he had run out of excuses. He knew he had driven his girlfriend away from him. Lately she hadn't been pushing him about seeing him that much. She seemed absorbed with something else. He didn't want to contemplate further. He knew he wouldn't like knowing. It was a fear he didn't want to run towards. He knew it wasn't always profitable to run towards fear.

In the first days he would lie to Cynthia that he was off visiting some friends or relatives, but he knew his fiancé wasn't buying into that anymore. But, he couldn't stop going to this place, like those good guide dogs trained by Pavlov... This place was outside their small town of Rusape, just off the road to Nyanga, about ten kilometres. It is a curve off the windward side

9

of the mountain, Nyarukwe Mountain. The horn of the mountain rising against the sky, the place is part of his namesake, John Borders' farm. This white man, John Borders, didn't bother that much with that part of his farm, so John was always safe there. In that unwanted part of the farm, John had found his other home. The other one was his girlfriend for over two years, Cynthia. Where he actually stays, in Vengere Township, the biggest township of Rusape, he never thought of that place as his home, even though he was born there by a lunatic pair of parents. They couldn't waste much of their time on their only child, but on weed and beer.

John had never gone to school beyond Vengere secondary school's second grade when his parents died. They had disappeared inside a car wreck, disappearing the way the wind moves- leaving no vacancy. John tried to swim away from himself but only reached the pool's end; he was absorbed into his parents' vices. He was a drug user, an acute user within the first year of their death, and now, his mood swings bordered on the lunatic, like his parents. He had graduated from being a weed user and was now into hard narcotics like cocaine and heroin. It was in abundant supply, he had a supply line from Mozambique, coming all the way from South American countries, Brazil and Colombia. The border between Zimbabwe and Mozambique was a watercolour border, so it was easier to get it through into Zimbabwe. Use of narcotics was the only way he stayed normal to himself. It was also a livelihood for him, but he was choosy in colleagues he would deal with. He had been lucky so far. The trade in narcotics had allowed him to keep his home in Vengere Township, and his fiancé. His place in the mountain was where he stored the drugs, and also his other secret. It was now only his doctor who knew about this secret.

"How do you feel when you are inside this box?" His doctor had asked him. *The casket looked vampire like- silent and motionless, waiting for its prey.* Doctor Muchena had accompanied John to this secret rendezvous, to be cocksure of what he was dealing with. He knew John was a user of hard narcotics, even though he had never questioned him, in the interview; they had had a couple of days before. He knew the signs, but he also knew it went deeper than that. He was shocked to realize it was that bad, because John had always maintained a normal façade, all his life. He knew him when he was a small child, and now, he assumed he was thirty something. He never thought there was something darker with the young man, only that he had wasted a good educational head by leaving school that earlier on.

"Doctor, when I am inside this casket and grave, I feel like a dead person. I become dead. It's like mocking death- a mock funeral for me. I will be attempting to get in touch with my parents. I want to find answers why they were the people they were. And, I can only get in touch with them if I go where they went. I had to construct this casket myself. It has this soft blanket inside, so that I could even spend the whole night asleep in it, communing with the dead. Sometimes I do spent three or so days lying inside this casket, talking to people from beyond, talking with my friends, my parents long since dead, and when I am inside this place, I feel secure, unafraid, at home."

"And, what have you talked of, with the dead, with your parents, John?"

11

"I have talked to several dead people…but my parents don't want to answer my questions, doc."

"Do you see them, your parents?"

"Yes, I do, all the time. I see them smoking their favourite weed…"

"Which is?"

"Marijuana, didn't you know they used that?"

"I suspected…so you said they have not been answering you, so what are you now thinking of doing, since they are still ignoring you?"

"I have been thinking of taking it further than that…"

"How further, John?"

"I am not sure, yet, doc." He said it in an offhand way. But the doctor knew what further action would come from all that, so he stalled him, a bit, "Do you love your girl, John?"

"Cynthia, yes, I do, doctor!"

"Why can't you tell her of this?"

"She would leave me."

"Maybe she might help you, you never know?"

"I can't face telling her of this, doctor."

"I could help you on how to divulge such information to her. We could do simulation of it, but not here. Let's go back to my offices and try to do that."

"Would it help, doctor?"

"Yes!"

Doctor Muchena was confident in his replies, even though he knew he was now running against the tide. John was gone too much into this crazy lunatic world of his, and to get him out of it was going to be difficult, especially if he fails to convince or encourage him to open up to his girl. He knew he also had to work through loopholes in the law of the land that didn't allow forceful containment, to forcefully take John to a better facility in Harare, over 200kms. He needed time to work the legal system. His girl, Cynthia, was his only hope for now, but he knew he couldn't rush it altogether. He didn't want to push John over the edge with a rash action. He was happy John had come with him. He needed some couple or so days to stall him. They returned together to the town centre, at his small offices, on the corner of Mutare Road and Nyanga Road. After giving him sodium valproate, and he had stabilized a bit, he had started talking to him about his life, his parents, his girlfriend, Cynthia. He didn't have lithium carbonate which was strongly linked to a reduced risk of suicide, self-harm and death in people with bipolar disorder, so he used the talking session with John, to push him away from what he intended to do.

"What do you really want in life, John?" He continued probing him, when he had stabilised mind. All the while they had been talking, and the doctor had worked around this issue. He wanted to find what solid ground was in John's ever-shifting psychotic mind. He wanted to focus on it, to emphasise on that. They had talked about his parents, his Vengere home, his work as a drug pusher, everything including Cynthia. He wasn't sure it was about Cynthia, so he had tried to focus him with a direct question.

"All I want to be is to belong to someone, to something, doc." So, the doctor emphasised about Cynthia, in his response, "Cynthia belongs to you...you belong to Cynthia, John."

13

"Yes, I love her, doctor" Doctor Muchena knew that wasn't enough. John loved his parents, as well. Does he belong to them, no! He has to feel he belongs to someone, to Cynthia, not just loving her.

"You could think of her as your home, John." He tried to encourage him along this thinking.

"I will disappoint her, doctor."

"You can't be sure of that without trying, John."

"You mean I should marry her, doctor?" *Why not, if he really means it*, mused the doctor? It would solve the situation for him, so the doctor asked him, "Do you want to do that, John?"

"Maybe…I want to be with her now." Hunger for Cynthia hits John like a painful pang.

"Now?"

"Yes, now, doc" He was sure of this.

"Ok, but please let me know how you are doing, and how Cynthia is when you see her."

"Yes, I will, doctor."

Doctor Muchena released John. He knew John was stabilised for the time being, so he knew there was no reason for him not to see the night out safely. When John returned to his Vengere home, he found his way to Cynthia's place. It was on the outskirts of Vengere Township, so by the time he arrived, it was dark, at around seven in the evening. Thus, he arrived unannounced to find himself confronting an unplanned, unpleasant sight. Cynthia had her new boyfriend with her, making out in her parents' small backyard. John confronting this in a stabilised state of bipolar send him on Nyanga Road, to his reliable home, in the Nyarukwe Mountains. The deepening evening clothing itself in shadows,

14

quieting the echoes of his footsteps, the only dirge he could hear was of the grass singing. The stars up the skies had no name, some were bright, cold bright, bright as frost, and others were faint, feeble pale, hardly there, like him. But this time he knew what to do. The whole world was always lying to him, lying that darkens the truth; it was the same world that had lied to his parents, now they are since gone, and no longer bother to talk to him. He had to find them to break this anguish of silence in him.

He had been hearing his cell phone beeping and he knew it was doctor Muchena who was trying again to tie him back to the lying world, so he couldn't answer it. He ignores it as he takes a strong rope; tie it to a strong brunch. There is a big to do for some several minutes as he creates a very strong loop on this rope, throw all his clothes, the cell phone, still beeping incessantly, into the casket. He climbs the tree, secures the rope's loop around his neck. When it is tied secure around his neck, he jumps into mid air. Blinding pain comes crushing on his mind like a cigarette butt' crash, under heavy boots. As he struggles to hang in mid air, he sees Cynthia making out with her new boyfriend, he sees his doctor lying to him that he would be fine, he sees his cocaine enveloped life passing through him, he sees the same lying world telling him that he is just a failure, not a victim, not a sufferer, not a patient; telling him to shut up, he sees his parents...

At first, he sees them as if he is waking up from a dream, lucid and still alive; remembering though not quite knowing what it is he knows. In that far away, they were two strangely solemn silhouettes, coming to him, telling him, with their looks, their gestures; that they are disappointed with him. He tells them he is

15

proud of them. The only thing John is proud of now is his parents. They faced this lying world all the best they could. He asks them to come nearer him. They come and stand below him, he sees into their faces, their eyes, they are not happy with their lives. He sees they are lost. They have the lost look they used to have when they were alive. In a constricted voice, he asks them.

"Why are you so unhappy?" And his father replies him,

"We wish we had tried a little bit more, to be normal, to live moral lives. We are disappointed we failed you. We wanted you to try a lot harder than us, and that's why we never talked to you when you tried to talk to us, in your attempts to reach us."

"But, I wasn't happy back there, Father..., and that's why I killed myself. The world out there lied to me, even Cynthia lied to me, Father."

"Cynthia is not important. It's you who should have been important to your life, John. There is nothing that makes a person think he is a victim more than being a victim, John" His father answers him.

"How so, father?"

"It doesn't matter how you were mistreated by the system, or even other people. its how you try to still work, to function, in a difficult environment, that should get you through it, John." His mother answers him this time. It is even difficult to contemplate all that wisdom, especially coming from his mother who had always seemed lost in real life. Such depth he had never related with his mother. Deep down he finds time and new dreams that would open up forgotten realms of creativity, so he finds resolve in himself. He has to be stronger for his parents, for himself. He wants to try a lot harder. He wants to reach his throat and untie

16

the rope. He tells himself he can do it. He tries to pull his arms, like gathering tension on loose ropes, but he can't raise his hands. They stay down there hanging limply like lazy loops, down there.

"But, it's now too late, mother." He comes to this sad realisation.

"Maybe it isn't...supposed it isn't, what are you going to do if you were given another opportunity, John?" He thinks he has replied to himself that, "Maybe, I will try to do things differently", he doesn't know...he doesn't know about a lot of things now. He knows he can't even face having a life without Cynthia, let alone having any other life than the one he has had. He isn't so sure of a lot of things now. He isn't even sure he is still talking to his parents. He isn't even sure he has said the things he is thinking he has said.

"You will know, my son." His mother seems to assure him, in his confusion.

"I will never know...I am dying, mother."

"No, you are not dying, John. I am sorry for hurting you." It is his mother, *is that his mother*, speaking in Cynthia's voice? The Cynthia he doesn't like anymore, maybe it is the trick of his mind, but he doesn't have an ability, anymore, to reply to her. To tell his mother that she shouldn't imitate the voice of that traitor. He just stares at her. She looks exactly like Cynthia. She is so sorry; she is crying and urging someone else, who is in a hurry, in the tree, climbing it. He looks at her again, stares harder at her and tells her she failed him. Even though he is silent, even though no words manage to reach his ears, he tells her everything was over between them. He would never try again. His parents failed him, too. And then, everything is falling down. The world is whirling

17

and whirling. Before he touches the ground, darkness envelopes him, absorbing him, it is now his home.

He doesn't hear the voice of Cynthia as she cries at his corpse, hitting the casket like kindling, making it close off, of itself on him, burying him into his home. He doesn't hear doctor Muchena saying he wanted to try to beat the fingers of death, thus had cut the rope, rather than wasting time trying to untie him slowly. That, he had always been running hard against time all the time with John, that he feels sorry he couldn't help him. Everything is nothing; he has entered the world of nothingness, not negation, no. Just nothingness!

John was the son of immigrants from Malawi, so there were no relatives to help them decide on where to lay his remains. Doctor Muchena and Cynthia were the only people who knew John on a personal level, so between them they decided what to do with his corpse. They processed his papers and buried John in his casket, in his grave, with most of his things, under the Nyarukwe Mountains.

SHE IS DEATH

She is a tiny girl. She is a waif, a whelp little thing, and picturesque like Penelope Cruz. She sometimes laughs at her own frame as her two hands almost circle her waist. She wonders what guys would be thinking of, as they circled her waist, a tigress crouching? Does that really excite them? She is fascinating; she knows that... she knows it makes them howl with want. She is now a woman. She feels she is now a woman. She has always been aware of her femininity, even when she was a little girl.

At one time she entered a modelling contest which she won, when she was barely 13, against older girls. She has always been full of passion for life; she has always lived in front of her own camera. She is not afraid of letting her camera zoom in on her and truthfully record her life. She is nineteen. She is fragile, she knows it, but she has always tried to live without fear. She talks a lot, maybe she realises nobody takes her seriously, because of her smallness, thus undaunted, she always talks. Her mouth seems always clotted in words. She suffers in the insides; she has deep fears inside of her. She lives with a high blood pressure complication. It courses through her blood, violently when she is disturbed. Her chest becomes a typhoon as she feels swooning, painful. She is fragile...breathless, shaking as if being disassembled. She can't really describe the pain. She breathes shallowly like a broken thing, thrashes like kindling, ungathered that way. She gasps for air as she chocks, and then everything is darkness...

19

She doesn't eat well nowadays. She used to think she suffers from anorexia nervosa, but she now understands better. But, she has what every model would fight for without fighting for it, really...her fabulous metabolism, and a fabulous body. Sometimes she wished she had the body without the blood pressure complications. She doesn't like it when she collapses and life stops for her. When she comes to she has to nudge herself, her mind. She has to tell her mind she has lost out on the things that have been happening since she fainted. It's like some form of death to her. So, she thinks she is death.

She has realised there are days when she was dead. If she were to collate all those moments when she was out they would add up to days. They could even make many weeks. She doesn't know what kind of life to bestow to those days when she was death. Were they hot days; were they cold, were they raining, or dry? How about the wind, what wind? What were people thinking of when she was out? It is always this that troubles her. But it is even larger than that. She is afraid one day she will collapse and never wake up from that. It is this that obsesses her. She knows she is a broken down, overused old engine, and that there are no parts to fix it. She knows she was born like that.

When, some few years ago, she started having those bouts of dying, she visited the doctor. She remembers the doctor telling her of her condition. He was a family doctor so he was kind to her. He told her she doesn't have to give up, to worry a lot. There were a lot of people living with that condition she had. He told her she was born with this condition, that it's an inherited thing, and that it's all about the genes. For some time after that, she

20

cursed her ancestors. She cursed herself for being weak to the extent of allowing those genes to mutate into her. Were her parents to blame? Her brother, sister, and parents don't have the same condition. Sometimes she wished it were something else…arthritis, allergies…etc, maybe. At least you don't have to worry or obsess about dying any day with these conditions. When she is dirty, sometimes, she tells herself she doesn't feel the dirty in her noses but the smell of death in her breathing. She calls them death's invisible fingers; after all, she is death. Yet, even though she knows she is fragile, she has always been strong. She tells herself she has to be strong.

The doctor told her she should avoid stressful situations, or any excessively exciting situations. But, she defies the doctor's advice. She feels she would be a pumpkin if she were to follow the doctor's advice to the dot. She doesn't want to be lonely. She wants to live. So, she goes out often. She tries to be happy. The thing she avoids is stressful situations. When her parents or relatives fight, and she is around, she would simply leave home or the place, walk a bit, or visit friends until she feels better. If it is at night, she would go to sleep, raise the volume of the radio or plug some earphones into her ears and listen to soothing music. The music would blot out her parents foul voices, and seduce her to sleep. She has to survive. She would like to defy that cruel ancestor who passed down to her this condition. She wants to live to see old age. Her thoughts have that power. She tells herself that she has the power to change the structure of her cells. After all she has made several pacts with death. She is now death herself.

21

THREE BROTHERS NEXT DOOR

Lovemore was dark, so dark. It's not right to use black, black is black. Anything different has always been black, isn't it? But, all that you could see at night was his smiles and eyes. Even at daylight it's his smiles and eyes that sparkled on his face. He had a very bright smile, but he always dressed like a communist- sparingly. His young brother, Joseph; was just as dark but mostly it was because he didn't bath regularly. He was scruffy. He wore scruffy things, not because he couldn't afford better clothing. He was always smelly, smelling sour, like vomit. But we had got used to his smelling. Nobody made fun anymore about it. The two had a cousin. He was always smart, unlike Joseph, and sweet most of the times. It was when people made fun of him, of his eye, that Calvin became angry, despondent and bitter. His left eye was destroyed. It licked a creamy substance. He was always with a handkerchief, a cloth, to clean this creamy thing coming out of his eye. In moments when he was despondent, a day or so after he had to deal with some cruel joke about his eye, he sometimes told us, and he was so quiet like life before people, that the eye was destroyed by a stepfather who hated him so much.

The stepfather would beat him whenever he was drunk, and verbally abuse him when he rarely was sober. Until he couldn't stand it anymore, he left home the night the stepfather destroyed his eye, through being beaten with a metal rod. He would say the

22

eye just cracked open and the seeing and blood matter oozed out. As he said this, his words would wind down low like his batteries had stopped. For some time nobody said anything...gutted, devastated. The pain we were feeling with him couldn't be localised. Our memories would balk at the task of finding the right words to console him with, but we learned how to do that.

He couldn't stay any longer home, after that beating. He was barely thirteen when that happened. He drifted through the villages, bushes and mountains, and towns. A year later, he found himself in Masvingo city where he stayed for a year working odd jobs, still sleeping rough. After a year in Masvingo he found his way to Chitungwiza. He found his way to his cousins in Zengeza Township. He also found his way next door. To those cousins he hadn't seen all his life. He had heard about them from his mother who stayed back with the abusive stepfather, in Zaka East, in rural Masvingo. They were his cousins on the mother's side. In finding his cousins he had started finding his way to sanity.

In Svosve Street, sitting by the gully besides the road, we helped him in finding his way to sanity. In those days we could spent the whole day sited in the gulley, watching girls passing bye, sometimes making fun at the girls, sometimes enjoying the girl's summer legs, shining so sweet in the falling sun. He never did that, but he always kept company with us, faithful, as trusting. Rarely, he laughed at the jokes, but most of the times, he was just a silent spectator. Our making fun at the girls helped him, somehow. He understood he was not the only person people would joke at. He could now let some of the jokes about his eye

23

pass without making a scene. He understood humanity needed some of those jokes for it to feel better with itself.

What he didn't like was being excluded, being ignored, being patronised by us. We had eventually got used to be around him. We could get into contact with the fluids from his eye without bunching, without even a blind bit of notice of it. We could also shake hands with him without any qualms. We knew he was harmless, we didn't even remember it smelled. We knew the liquid was a harmless stream, that there were no crocodiles beyond the surface. We understood why he was generally cleaner and tidier than the rest of us. It was a constant ritual with him, to be clean. We loved him, anyway.

A couple of years later, Calvin and his brothers, Lovemore and Joseph, left our area for the Seke Suburb, Unit D. They left to stay in another suburb of Chitungwiza, a bit away. We begin to let go of them. We couldn't see them regularly afterwards. Eventually we drifted apart.

Later, Lovemore died, and they say that he died of AIDS. Joseph has been ill for years, dying slowly from multiple myeloma, a cancer of the bone marrow. It's not curable; the cancer cells ceaselessly eating into the bones, dissolving them into empty small holes, expanding, like a pointillist painting. Even though chemotherapy could have given him some time, but he couldn't even afford it, to begin it.

We haven't heard anything about Calvin, though. Some say he left the country for Botswana. They say it was five summers ago when he left.

A note for the Ocean City Girl: R.I.P

Gift, my younger brother came from our rural home yesterday, to tell me that she was since gone. Gift said it was now over 3 months since the Ocean City Girl had died. Of course, I had heard she was ill. Nyasha, a friend from long ago, told me that her husband had died five years ago of AIDS, and that he had infected her with the disease, and that her only kid with John, her husband, was the first to die before John's death. Nyasha is an old mutual friend; and he had told me all that a year ago, but I didn't know I should have come into her world and disturb it again. She was staying in another town, Marondera town, so I just couldn't meet her in the streets. I could have visited, it is only 75km from Chitungwiza city where I stay, but I don't know I should have done that.

I don't even know, whether on her death bed, she remembered there was this sultry petulant young man in her life, years back then. It is now 18 years since I last laid my eyes on her. The sad realisation now is to know that I will never ever do that again in this life. She is gone. But, I remember her nevertheless. I remember her; she called herself the Ocean City Girl. She was a younger sister to Celine. Celine who had loved me: and I had been a pain-some bastard and left her.

She had said, when I left Celine; that she and Celine viewed me with so much contempt, that I should feel personally deserving of it. But, I was surprised when she accepted my date afterwards. She later told me that she accepted my date request because she wanted to hurt me in the same way that I had hurt

26

her sister. She sure took all the pleasures in making my world into such a hell-hole.

She hatched for a vengeful relationship straight away. Like a sucker for trouble, I fell badly in love with her. With her, I went all the way. Was I unconsciously trying to atone for the wrong I had done to her sister? She liked it. She became a woman insane, murdering me every moment she could.

It's on a Sunday, the Sunday I am bringing her home for the first time. My Father is home from his workplace in Mutare city. I have been staying in Harare for a year or so now. Since I came home for the holidays, we are seeing each other a lot. Everyone knows about this relationship although nobody approves of it. This is one thing that is hard for her. There is nothing I can do about it because I don't want to let her go. Part of her wants to let me go in order to please other people, but another part is falling in love with me. I know that my own parents don't like her but I don't really care this time.

I am in the high adrenalin of a relationship. Although my parents don't approve our relationship, they try to be polite with her. After spending some time with my siblings, I walk her back to her place. She starts complaining that my parents don't like her. I lie that they like her fine. She says that even her family don't approve of the relationship. She also says that her sister is angry with her. I tell her that there is nothing I can do about it. We argue. She says that we should stop seeing each other. I refuse to let her go. She says that it is over and leaves me for home. I can't let her go like that. So, I follow her. I am begging, I am telling her that I am not accepting this. I am on my knees and

27

I am telling her that I love her, and that she loves me and that that's all that matters.

We haggle about this for about two hours and we are standing close to where her village, Gwanyan'wanya, hugs my village, Mapfurira. I tell her that I am not letting her go home until we sort this thing out. I tell her that if she leaves me, then I would follow her to her home. She realizes that I am serious about this. So, she tells me that I should not go back to Harare the morrow day. We could sort the problems tomorrow afternoon. She says that she needs to sleep on things. I accept the proposal because I know I can't push her any further than I have already done.

The next day, my parents are surprised when I tell them that I am not returning back to Harare that day. I see her, the Ocean City Girl, in the afternoon, when she is coming back from the shops. There is nothing we talk of, about this issue. She just laughs it off and tells me that she was only trying to figure out how much I love her. I laugh the things off with her too. We are laughing and new to each other- we forget about all the fights. We kiss each other hard; we are teenagers in someone's dark basement, bodies pressed together like we are one person, one large person. But it is broad daylight, and nothing seems the matter with us, but nothing improves either. We are always fighting after this, losing particular. It is a game of dress-up with her, everything is imagined. She knows everything about me, but don't show any desire to meet me across this bridge that I have been trying to build, as if she is waiting to find something else more about me. She also seems to know what she would do if she fails to find the things she is looking for.

28

But, I continue to enter this bend knowingly. I learn it the harder way, why I shouldn't just enter bends without analyzing things first. Now, I would rather have bends planned and straightened, not curvy before I enter them. Back then, even though I knew she was simply bad business, I couldn't stop. She became the first woman who broke my heart. And, it was difficult girls that I was scared of afterwards. But, I couldn't let her go. I kept holding onto her, even though pain was all that I was getting from that relationship.

And later, it's another day, in September 1994. I have come back home for her. I received a letter from her, a couple of months before, that I replied but she never wrote back. In the letter, she had cut it off with me again, citing that I was useless, that I wasn't working, and that I wasn't even going to school to further my education. I have come to meet her as she is coming from the shops where she went to buy groceries. It is spring, so it is a beautiful sunny day, but she is with Wellington Nyanguru. I don't like this guy. All that he had been doing was to disturb me from seeing her, all through our 8 months old relationship. I know he was put to that task by John Samaboreke he is friends with, who was her other boyfriend. I know that but I don't want to confront her about this guy. Wellington's job is to disturb me, to make my life a hellhole. It's good with her because she doesn't know what to do with me. After all, I am a failure in her eyes, for I have not amounted to anything after school, and this new boyfriend of hers is at the University. In her eyes, I am simply a failure. She is using this Wellington fellow to staunch me off of her, but I have always wanted to fight for things that I feel someone is refusing me unfairly, that I feel so much for. I am

29

going to see her this day, anyway. I am waiting for her where the two roads from Nyatate branch off, one going through the village, and the other one going through the fields. Then she arrives and, she is with this Wellington fellow. I ask to see her.

She says, "I am not seeing you, John." I ask her, "Why not?"

She says, "I have no business with you." Her breath crackles on the dryness of September's hot air.

I say, "We are dating, so, I have business seeing you."

She says, "You are forcing yourself back into a relationship with me, John. I told you in the letter that I don't want to be with you." And, I counter,

"We need to discuss things, then."

She says, "Say whatever you want to say, John." Her left hand grabs her waist, and the right hand is flashed up in a talk-to-my-hand gesture, lush caves of her body calling out to me- in anger her mouth is pouted. I want to hold her in my arms and cool her fierce beauty but I also want this Wellington to disappear. I ask this Wellington fellow to leave us alone. He refuses. She also says,

"You can say whatever you want to say in his presence." I say,

"No! He should first leave." I knew with this Wellington out of the way, I could get to cool her, and get us headway to first base, and with a bit of luck, second base, maybe.

He says he is not leaving. We shout at each other with this Wellington, and she joins in on his side. It is a shouting match for the three of us now. It is like the ocean's waves at high tide with no hindering breakwaters, coming crashing on the shore of a populated city, an ocean city. She was, after all, the Ocean City Girl! In her anger, she tells me that she is seeing the friend of Wellington, my namesake, a certain John Samaboreke, of the

30

Chihobvu Village. I already knew about this, but I am boiling with anger.

I ask her, "Why have you been keeping this from me." And, she tells me that she told me the reason, a long time ago- that she was entering into this relationship with me to revenge for her sister, the way I mistreated her sister. I am furious with her so I hold her talk-to-me hand in mine, telling her I won't leave her until we discuss the things and come to an understanding. What I am saying with this is that until she had given in and took me back. She tries to wriggle her hand out of mine, but I am gripping her hard. She starts crying with anger. She is spiting saliva all over my face, calling me a pig. I am furious with her for calling me a pig and spitting on my face but I keep holding her hand, anyway. I am doing this because I also want to provoke this Wellington to get involved so I would find a reason to beat him up, but he is clever enough to understand the challenge. He stays out of this fight.

When she realises that I am not letting her go, she bites my hand hard like a savage animal, and it hurts real bad. Instantly, I am profusely bleeding. I let go her hand. The pain on my hand is good enough pain to staunch the pain in my heart. I have always used another pain to deal with a pain I don't know how else to deal with. I am no longer angry with her. I am depleted, subdued. I know I won't beat her. I don't want to beat her. I have never beaten a woman, all of my life. Honour must really have something to do with a person you love. I let her go with total misgivings, about me, my life. I am a looser. This is the last time I see her. I walk so slowly, so lost, like a weevil creeping in, is what my life's about. I don't tell people at home that I was hurt by her.

31

I just lie I got injured somewhere else. I am dealing with double pain.

Now, I remember the waste of pain that comes with the breakdown of a relationship. That day, loss loomed big like the sun eclipsed by the moon. For years after that it seemed to me there was nothing after the first heartbreak and love. It was with the Ocean City Girl that I wanted to search for something special together that I probably thought was there in relationships. From that moment onwards, I started to cut sorrows, shaping a shape that I had learned of without knowing. And, I could only watch them; one girl after another, coming into my life and getting carried away by the "me" that I did not understand.

Now, remembering the names of those ex-girlfriends is difficult for me as their names were names of a crash-test, dummies without nuances or meaning. My restlessness always toppled them into fallen beauty.

But, despite all the angst between us she never stopped calling me dear; I didn't know what that meant. But, it is the flower she left me with in my heart, even now as I think of her. I thought she loved me but no, she didn't. Maybe she did in her curious way. In spite of everything, I was still dear to her. In the diary that I kept, I extract the quote from the letter, when breaking up with me, she wrote to me; she said, "But dear, bear in mind that your actual future lies on your physical and mental identity. I wish you everything that life could offer you, especially the best and the most beautiful." She wasn't one of those best and most beautiful things in life she wished for me. In her grave now, I hope it is not night dark, but a soft twilight, that she is happy. I hope to God that wherever she is now she has found rest and that she isn't angry with me anymore.

Rest in peace, the Ocean City Girl!

WHEN HE WAS STILL CLOSER HOME

He was barely two years old, he was told. His mother told him about all this for he doesn't remember anything of that time. His mom says when he was two years he was such a lonely child. Such independence even makes him now wonder, a lot. She says he refused to go to the fields with her and his older brother, Munhuwumwe, during summer cropping months.

"Rhayi mwanangu, let's go to the fields now," she would say.

And he would refuse,

"No!" She would have to force him,

"You will be abducted by Vanamupakatsine." Vanamupakatsine are muti-killers, who would kill people, especially young children, and take their body parts to mix it with *muti* (roots or trees) medicines. They would put this mixture, usually in the walls or foundation floors of their shops or businesses premises. These were thought to increase flow of customers into their business, thereby growing the business.

When his mother does that, Rhayi would cry. He was angry with his mother for trying to push him, using fear.

"Hosara hangu pano." "Hosara hangu pano." He is not afraid of Vanamupakatsine, so he would be saying, "I will stay home alone." "I will stay home alone."

When his mother realises that she could never pluck him off home, she would cook a lot of porridge for him, a pot's full of it. She would leave it outside the kitchen, behind the kitchen where he would be playing. He would have an assortment of toys; bricks, logs, etc..., to construct his dreams with. He would play

34

alone at their homesteads, creating roads, railway lines, airlines, in his dreams; constructing some path to wherever he thought his playing-with-things could take him to. The sky behind him is blue, improbably blue, the eastern skies' blue- he wants to fix it a bit, put some clouds, a low swarm of birds, crows about to peck each other. Sometimes his mind would make him do that. His mother and Munhuwumwe would be at the fields, working. The fields were slightly over a kilometre from home, but he wouldn't bother being left behind. He would play a bit, and when he was hungry, he would open his pot of porridge, and eat it using his own hands as a spoon. Then take his afternoon sleep, wake up late afternoon, and still play, until they come back. When he was that younger, time seemed to run errands for him, he revered in it. Sometimes he would play alone for a full day, the birds, locusts, and in the evening, the crickets around him doing their own chores.

Growing up was difficult for some time, trying to connect with others of his age. He always preferred to be alone, constructing stuff, especially in his mind. He learned the art of entertaining himself, that earlier on in his life, so it wasn't difficult to retreat into his mind's dream worlds. Rhayi grew up fast as he tried to connect with others. He became very, very mischievous. He felt he was trying too harder to connect, to be normal, to compensate for those lonely early life years. He would live, even in those mischief-making episodes, in strange places. A lot of people couldn't understand him. Even his mom couldn't understand him. She felt he was a pain in the ass for her. He exasperated her with his mood swings and temperament, so he did to all those he

35

played with, mostly his sisters. Later; elders, teachers, even the headmaster at his schools didn't know what to do with him. But he was good at his studies, and always made the top 5 easily. He seemed like he had come from a world they didn't know how to deal with, sometimes as if he had come from that world unwilling, and that he was now trying to return back to that world. He couldn't understand why they all thought he had to behave the way they wanted him to do. He wanted to be someone else, or somewhere else. His mother would sometimes tell him that he almost killed her during pregnancy. It would make him feel so guilty.

When his mother was pregnant with him, she told him, she was very ill, most of the times anyway. That he was a very difficult pregnancy. He wanted to ask her,

"Did I ask to be that", but he couldn't do that to her.

She said most of the times she felt so hot, so ill, and she would spent a lot of time naked. Sometimes she would say; it's an uncle who wanted to kill her through this pregnancy. He would wonder why this uncle waited to do that on him, not on Munhuwumwe, or even his sisters, later. His mom became so ill when it was time to give birth to him. She was sweating, painful, frustrated... It was on Monday, 12 July 1973 when she really hit the deep end. She was later ferried by a relative, Sekuru Nyadundu, to Mt Mellery Hospital, just below the Nyanga range of mountains.

It was when she started feeling as if he really wanted to kill her, in that Monday night; she tried to ask the uncles and grandma to take her to the Nyadundu's residency, in the middle of this night. They said she should stay home, and that grandma

36

would be the midwife, if she were to enter into labour. Grandma, Rhayi's paternal, was so good at midwifery, and her services were in huge demand in their village and the surrounding villages, so she didn't have to worry. But deep down her bones, she felt it was a futile move, she knew he was going to kill her.

That night she walked to Nyadundu's residency, without much on her. She was very ill, and Rhayi now thinks it was mental. It is a distance of one and half kilometres, but she managed it. Nyadundu was surprised to see his sister; he called her that, in the middle of the night- fully pregnant- pretty much naked and ill, at his place. He gave her Mai Nyadundu's clothes to wear and took her to the hospital, about 20 km away, where on the morning, now Tuesday, at about 6am, 1973, 13 July, his mother managed to give birth to him. She would say it was this pregnancy that broke her, that it took a lot from her as she pushed and pushed harder for him to get out. That he seemed not to want to get out. Sometimes he wonders; it would make him think, what if he had totally refused to get out of her, what was she going to accuse him of? How would she have felt about it all? Was he going to be happy, if he had stayed out there?

Maybe that could be the reason why he was such a difficult child to deal with. His childhood was difficult for his mom, as well. When he was still a tot, his mother would say, he made her life miserable. Just after birth, she said, his chest was swelling, growing big, as if stuff inside him- the heart, lungs.., were growing too fast, thus pushing his chest out. He had huge breathing problems then. He still has a big chest...he thinks it's the diaphragm line that bulged, such that he slouches backwards when walking, rather than frontwards, like all tall people would

37

normally do. Sometimes people make this protruding diaphragm some jokes, calling it a protruding stomach.

Yes, his stomach now protrudes, but it is due to growing old- a sagging middle, flapping cellulite. He doesn't have problems with his chest anymore. He remembers it was a difficult chest, growing up, in actual fact; it was too heavy for him to carry. Sometimes he would breathe shallowly, but nowadays it is okay. He has always wondered what if there is something wrong inside there, that's still waiting for its time to manifest itself into something life-taking. When it comes back, he obsesses, would it take him back to that place he had come from. He always seems to want to go back there.

His mother would sometimes blame his uncle. Maybe that's why Rhayi became so mischievous; he was trying, maybe misguidedly, to defy all that. To defy the uncle who seemed to want to do wrong to him. Resentment percolates, it makes people ugly, and he still doesn't like that uncle. Maybe he was trying to learn to love someone else, other than his mother; thus in trying to connect he resorted to mischief. Maybe it was her way of trying to control his mischief. Maybe she loved him more, and she would say, "More than she had ever loved anyone in all her life".

"What of her husband, his father", he wondered.

Sometimes she would enjoy the mischief, as long as she was not the object he would be working on, as long as he works on people she doesn't like, as long as the object of his pranks didn't come home to make a scene, she would laugh with him. She liked laughing at life. He loved laughing at life, at people, too.

38

***** ***** *****

When he was about six, when his mother was carrying his second sister's pregnancy. It was her fifth pregnancy, and so she was now calmer, in September, 1979. Rhayi and his first sister, the fourth child, Muneinazvo, were staying in Chitungwiza, at their family home, where he is still staying today. They were staying with their father, who worked in Harare. It was a day job so his father would leave enough food for the two, as he leaves for work, sometimes his father would cook evening relish in the morning, and leave for the workplace. He would tell them to keep at home, not to play outside. He didn't like confinement so he would invite all the kids of the street over to their home, make a party of the abundant food, including the evening relish, and they would have a feast of it.

Then he would take junk pieces, of broken-down cars, in the adjacent school's grounds, home to build his dreams, houses, cars, stuff... Sometimes he would take them inside the house. His father would first visit his mother, at Harare Hospital, at the maternity ward. His mother was waiting for the coming of this fifth child. His father would come home to find the home turned into a dumping ground. He would beat him, and then force him to clean the stuff up. But the morrow morning, Rhayi would do the same thing. His father had a terrible time with him.

Eventually his father stopped cooking a lot of food, especially evening relish, and could only leave enough to get them by, but Rhayi still invited the other kids over and would make do with the little they had.

At one time, it was the day his mom was coming home from the hospital. She had given birth to the fifth child, Tambudzai, without problems. She came home to be confronted by a yard full of parents of kids he had doctored *mhiripiri* (red-hot pepper) into their eyes. Telling them that he was an eye doctor, and that he was treating them of an eye disease he had just discovered. So, he would put grounded *mhiripiri* into their eyes and they would howl off in tears to their parents. He knew they were in unbelievable pain, but he was having great fun at it, at being the doctor.

His mother, even though she was weak from the pregnancy, had to perform to the best of her abilities to soften and talk these parents off their yard. She was cross with him but she was weak. She was looking weary, bags- actual pieces of luggage- under her eyes, were parked on her cheekbones. So, his father told him to go outside, into the adjacent school grounds to take a stick that he would beat him with. He went and took practically a big log that could have felled a big bull. His father thought he was joking, but he even tried to bring it into the house, with leaves and branches on it. His father stopped him. His father told him to sit in the kitchen as his mother prepared food for him, and that he would effect the punishment when he had finished eating. Rhayi sat quietly in the kitchen.

As his father got absorbed into the eating, of the delicious food his mother had cooked, Rhayi sneaked out of the kitchen, off home to the next street where there were kids he knew, and he played with these kids until it was a bit dark. He sneaked back home, ate, and went to sleep. His father was off to Nyatsime Beer Hall. When he returned he was drunk, and Rhayi was flat out

40

asleep. So his father couldn't wake him up to effect the punishment.

The morrow morning he left for work. His father knew his mother was now around, and she would figure out better ways to control him. His father didn't know how else to deal with him, other than beating him down, and their relationship was fractious, because of that. He didn't know how to love his father. He didn't like him. Back then, he knew, him and his father would go together like water and fire, him the fire, and his father the water. He wouldn't stop though, he would continue defying him. He would create more mischief, even on his mother, but he felt home making those pranks on his mother. Back then, his home was his mother.

To say he loved her, or that he loves his parents, don't get him anywhere closer to how he felt about her. He felt he was a part of her. He came from her. So he wouldn't know how not to love her. He doesn't even use the term; "I love myself", to describe the way he feels about himself. "I love myself", could only be a polarity of, "I don't love myself". How he feels about himself can't be put into words. How he loved his mother couldn't be put into words like, "Oh yeh, I love her". But that's all that he could only say to estimate how he felt. She was his home. He felt the same way about this home of his, his mother as his home, the way he felt about his love for his mother. For one to realise a "home", what it really represents, you have to be where you are "not at home", and then you can appreciate what a home is.

He was out of his mother's womb, but he knew he was still closer to his home, and that home still influenced him. He loved

41

that home. The battle was on staying very close to that home and maybe die to return back into it, or to try to move on, to live life, to find other homes. We do the second option the more we grow into our bodies, blood, puss, etc...

***** ***** *****

There were those years of the liberation war, about 1978-79. Nights of the *cluck, cluck* and *boom* of the bazookas, grenades, AK47s, in the fields and in the surrounding mountains. One such night they went to sleep, and it started around the mountains, off their fields to the west. The soldiers, liberation war soldiers, were in the mountains and Smith's Rhodesian soldiers were in the valley of Matimba. They would see, in this night, through gaps on their doors, bullets flying to and from these places. They were scared like hell, but they were with their mother, so it was okay. They knew she could protect them.

There were several days they could run off home into the open fields. Several days they would sleep at the fields. These open fields were safer from attacks than their home was, because none of the feuding fighters would have wanted an open war. Some nights they would leave home and the village for the next village, Gwanyan'wanya, which was sometimes removed from the fighting, and sleep at Mai Sabina Nyabocho's residence. But sometimes the war would spill into this village, so they would invade the nearby big and dangerous forest of Muchena Mountains. They would share it with an assortment of the big-foot family, the dangerous snakes, bite-some other animals. They did spent some time behind Matsungo's (Mawonapadi Shopping

42

Centre) place, which was on the fringes of this huge forest and mountains. And other days they ran deep into the forests into the meeting point between Nyajezi River and Nyangombe River. After some time, when the fighting had eased out, they would return home, at one time to find their homes razed to the grounds.

Their home was where the base of the liberators was. He remembers; he liked the *pungwes* (all-night vigils) they would have, once in a while. In those nights, they couldn't sleep, as well; seeing the soldiers and the Vanamujibhas (war collaborators) dancing, making out in twos, tumbling into soft grass, kissing, carousing, and having those untamed, wild parties of theirs. He wished he were older so he could make out with woman collaborators, who seemed so beautiful and unafraid.

It was one of those days they would run off into the adjacent fields nearby; he remembers there were four in their family, four kids in their family. His younger brother, the one behind him, had died in May 1978, and he just doesn't remember the death, or his funeral. He doesn't know, why. But he remembers him; or memories of him are alive during this time only when they were running off into the fields. He was holding his hand. Munhuwumwe was carrying their little sister, Muneinazvo. They were eating *Chimupoto hai* (maize-flour baked bread) with tea. So they would run-off with their food, eating whilst running. All the memories he has of that time have been of running off. This became his home, running (in or out, he never knew what was home, out or into this place he had called home). But his younger brother was there. His actual name was Norman, and it is this

43

memory that didn't run away with him into the fields and bushes and never returned.

His mother called Norman, and for some years, "Nyakuenda", meaning "The gone". Sometimes she would call him "Nyakuenda Wangu", meaning, "The gone, my beloved", trying he supposes, to make them all feel Nyakuenda belonged to her alone.

Everyone wanted to own him. His mom would sometimes tell him, to dispossess him off this brother that this brother was long since dead by the time they were running off into the fields. He couldn't argue with the past, especially a past he wasn't very sure of. She would say it was because of pneumonia. But Rhayi owned him anyway, as a brother he never got to really know. It's difficult to lose a child at that stage, and he thinks it affected his mother in ways he could never understand, so he always would allow her to own the memories of Nyakuenda, as her own. It would have been rude to say to his mother that Nyakuenda had gone back to where he came from, to his home. After all he had come from her womb. He could only have gone there.

It's Nyakuenda's death that would get his mom really, really worked up; crying, resentful, and full of anger at life, at everyone, even at herself. Maybe she blamed herself for his death. It would be a totally fucked-up mood she would be in and they wouldn't know what to do with her. She would tell them that Nyakuenda got really ill, and that she tried every medication she could think of. When his mother says she tried every medication she could think of, it meant simply that, he had come to know what that really meant when he got down with an ailment. She would push one medication after another on him until he wanted to just leave home. Her mother had learned, it seems, earlier on; how to deal with diseases on Nyakuenda. She knew every root, every leaf, every buck, and every soil, everything that could get someone well.

She had also taken Nyakuenda to the hospital where he was given some tablets, which she also religiously endorsed him with. She visited every N'anga (traditional faith healer) she could, every Christian faith healer, every Medicine person, but the boy got worse and worse. How it must have killed her, he can't even contemplate that. Nyakuenda could hardly breath, was sneezing, and was so frail. On the day he died, in the morning, after a very difficult night with him, she asked his uncles to take her to the hospital with the kid, and they refused. So, she carried Muneinazvo in her hands (Muneinazvo was barely a year old) and Nyakuenda on her back, and walked off to Mt Mellery.

She said she was singing and crying on the way, and sometimes humming off a tune to stop the two kids from crying. It was about 9 in the morning, at around Madindingwe Mountains when she met some distant relative on her way. Nyakuenda had been quite for some time, so she stopped to talk to this relative, who felt very sorry for her. The relative meant to check how Nyakuenda was when she found him; his face had turned to the colour of old used newspapers. She asked his mother to un-carry Nyakuenda, off her back; lying she wanted to hold him as she rested. When she had taken hold of Nyakuenda, she told her that Nyakuenda was gone.

His mother had this relative to console her, and the unsuspecting Muneinazvo. This relative helped her by carrying Muneinazvo back home, and she carried Nyakuenda, about ten

45

kilometres. She arrived home; midmornings to announce to the rest of the family that Nyakuenda had gone. Nyakuenda was on her back, gone. He supposes she had announced to all of them, including him, but he doesn't remember a thing about it all. This obsesses him.

Maybe he just closed off, he doesn't know anything. He still has this tendency of closing off, by getting inside himself, and work the thing out, until it becomes easy to hold inside him. But he would remember it afterwards. The problem is he just doesn't remember it, and funnily enough, he feels, it shaped him; misremembering Nyakuenda. He was told about Nyakuenda's death later, and he would remember that, the telling by his mother. His mother, when they were a bit older and he was about 7, would show him where Nyakuenda was buried, his actual grave. That grave still obsesses him, as well.

He would like to think it is the home Nyakuenda went to. If it is a home to Nyakuenda, it must be a home for him. He had come from the same womb with Nyakuenda, he felt his mother had buried her womb inside that grave, thus she had died with Nyakuenda. It must represent a home for him, too. Passing by this place, ever after that, it was some kind of a weird thing for him for he seemed to be the one encased in that grave, especially when he was passing through that grave place in broad daylight. At night he was afraid, especially when he was alone. Afraid Nyakuenda might decide to get out of the grave and say, "hello". He wouldn't know what he would say to that.

Their home is surrounded by graves of the liberation time, let alone the whole village or area, so there are many a story of ghosts illuminating the nights, he had heard or seen. He was afraid that someday this brother would decide he now wanted to introduce himself into his consciousness, to light up the dead memories. He would think the boy would wait for him in the road besides the grave and improves on the introduction by saying, "hello old brother. How are you doing? Do you now remember me?" He didn't even know whether this young brother had been growing up in the grave like he had been doing. Would it be an older boy's tenor voice or a teenager's freak bass voice? This road was the way to their gardens, and to where they would collect and sent off their cattle to the graze lands, so there was little avoiding of this place.

That earlier on, in his childhood years, he didn't really want to avoid it, he now realises, deep down he wanted, or wished, or even willed Nyakuenda could come back, and so, passing by this place, he thought he could provoke him to do the raising from the dead act on him. So that he would hold his breath, so tightly, supposing it was going to happen, but it doesn't. When he had passed the grave place that's when he would let it go, sometimes wistfully. And as he grew older, and when he had realised Nyakuenda wasn't coming back, this place ceased to call him to it. He started using other roads.

He now feels he got in touch with death, too early in his life, and he could deal well with the other deaths that came later in his life. But he still wished Nyakuenda was there with him. He grew up without a younger brother. His brother, Munhuwumwe, had him, but he didn't have anyone, so his younger sisters became the younger brother he didn't have. For Rhayi, it was something else...

47

***** ***** *****

He was very young when he started herding the cattle, goats and sheep, around when he was 4 or 5 years. He was always willing to do that. It was an activity that would still give him an opportunity to play whilst doing it- and he would play. It usually was in summer when he wouldn't enjoy this activity, of looking after or for the cattle. They had a bunch of very difficult cattle that had an undying knack to want to stray off.

In those summer months, they would wake up early, at around 4 in the morning, to go ploughing or cultivating the fields. It was usually a threesome pairing. When he was not herding the goats, sheep, cows, calves, and those cattle they wouldn't be yoking that day, he would be part of this threesome. The first person in this threesome would lead the yoked oxen (draught power), and it would usually be him, and Munhuwumwe would be the *Muchairi* (the one who urges the cattle on, so that they would pull the plough), and then babamunini, his uncle, would be the one guiding the plough, so that it would plough well.

He had three uncles. The one his mother hated, the one who seemed to want to kill him in pregnancy worked alone, with his own family. The second one, Uncle Kenneth, was the one they worked with most of the times, before he left with his family to the resettlement areas. Despite the fact that he was a difficult child, this uncle liked him anyways, and he would enjoy the mischief. The other uncle, Uncle Patrick, was a bit laid back and lazy, a mamma's boy. He didn't enjoy farm work, but fishing; and there, they would be buddies when it came to fishing. He would say, in a huge pencilled smile illegally crossing the borders of his

48

face, "Let's go fishing, Rhayi", and Rhayi wouldn't wait a moment to think. It was a big "Yes, uncle". Rhayi liked fishing as he grew older...the dreams were even good as one stared at the gently flowing water, waiting for the hook to entice some unsuspecting fish. But back then, when he was still young, this uncle was cruel to work with.

Uncle Patrick always preferred to urge the cattle, and he had this long whip (leather whip). If you don't control the plough or cattle and leave some banks of land uncultivated or unploughed, he would swipe your back with the whip and it would pain like hell. Rhayi was always the woolgatherer, so he always got on the wrong end of that whip. This uncle would make jokes about it, saying he does a, "Chiwepu pamunhu, chiwepu pamombe", meaning, "a whip on the person, a whip on the cattle".

Rhayi hated it, and didn't like to work with him. He thought this uncle did this intentionally, so that nobody would want to work with him, thus nobody would bother him to go to the fields. Sometimes, if you play with his things, he would beat you like he was beating an older person, and sometimes Rhayi's mother didn't like it. She would fight this uncle, and later when his father comes home on weekends, and hear of this, he would also beat this young brother of his, thereby angering grandma, who protected this uncle, her last son. Home would become so fractious and tense.

This uncle had mental problems and sometimes when his wires, inside his head, touched wrongly, he would go haywire and beat people around, even his mother and grandma. They were really scared of him when the moon was full in the skies and things got muddy-fouled-up in his head.

But Uncle Kenneth took to Rhayi's pranks differently. It was usually mid-day when Rhayi would take the cows and the yoked off cattle to the graze lands, a bit removed from the fields. Once he gets there he would instantly drift through the mazes of his dreams, dreaming and dreaming... He would find a particularly nice, warm place and it was usually in the gully, sheltered by big trees, with some very beautiful sands. He would play alone, or just dream, or just think. He would create his wonderful dreams, worlds that had nothing to do with his life, then. Eventually he would fall asleep.

When he wakes up, its hours later, and he would check, just around this place for the cattle. They had drifted whilst he was asleep, he doesn't know where to. He would simply create a story as he goes home empty of the cattle. When he arrives home, he would have his story with him. He was a dreamer, so stories were not difficult for him to create. He would arrive home, and he was so hungry he could eat a live dog. Sometimes people had just finished eating the afternoon meal and he would like to do the same.

"Where are the cattle, young man?" Uncle Kenneth would ask him, whilst Uncle Patrick proceeded off to his hut, chuckling to himself; because he knew what was going to happen. Rhayi was supposed to bring the cattle back with him, as he returned for his afternoon meal, and it's obvious to everyone, including Uncle Kenneth what had transpired. But he was prepared for that.

"I don't know." He would answer, as if the possibility of finding an answer to this problem was a problem itself.

"How can you say you don't know, were you not the one looking after them, Rhayi?"

"I was uncle. But when I entered the gully looking for Jamaica (one of the troublesome cattle), when I got out of the gully, after failing to find him, I found out all the other cattle had disappeared. I looked around for them but could not find them." To his mind, in this infinite universe of his mind, all things were mathematically possible, even certain.

"You are lying, young man. Cattle don't just disappear into thin air like demons. Where did you look around for them?"

"I went to Haripo's fields, then to grandma's mountain, and then to the valley of Matimba, and came through Vhere's fields; and they were nowhere to be found."

"You are lying, Rhayi."

"No, I am not lying, uncle. You can even ask Baba Mudondo, he saw me looking for them. I am telling the truth. I swear, I am telling the truth, by the name of Nyakuenda." Uncle Kenneth wouldn't now waste time listening to him, but would swore by the name of his grandma, the great-grandma Mbuya Pfupi, and the light-skinned witch, Mbuya Makawore, who was the younger sister of Mbuya Pfupi, that if he were to find them in these places, he was going to beat him. He would leave for the graze lands and fields, looking for them. Rhayi wouldn't join his uncle in this endeavour, if not invited or forced. He would stay home and eat.

His Auntie, his Uncle's wife, would be teasing him as he eats, telling him that he slept or played, as usual, as the cattle strayed. She knew the truth, and everyone knew the truth, but he would refuse to be goaded. Everyone also knew how he was going to

51

get out of that, when Uncle Kenneth returns back with the cattle, and tells him,

"You were lying, young man. I found the cattle exactly in the valley of Matimba, where you said you checked for them."

If he didn't want to be bothered with a fight, he would just agree, and say when he checked there were not there, and that they must have been somewhere else, and had later strayed to those fields, or he would deny it completely. He would tell huge billowing lies.

"I never said I checked in the valley of Matimba." But his Uncle would insist,

"That's exactly what you said. You said you checked at Haripo's fields, then grandma's mountain, then to the valley of Matimba, and you came through Vhere's fields."

Uncle Kenneth would simply be pushing him, and everyone at home including his brother, Munhuwumwe; were waiting expectantly to hear what he would say to that; waiting, goaded in laughter. Rhayi would find his usual way out.

"No, I didn't say that, Uncle. I said I looked for them at Aaron Mapfurira's fields, and then to Mandeya's fields, then to Mandiopera's fields, and then I came home."

Uncle Kenneth would raise his eyes in disbelief, not believing one word he was hearing. The others can't control the giggling, the laughter. Rhayi would enforce his new position by saying,

"How do you suppose, Uncle, I could check the places you have said I checked without including Mandiopera's fields, knowing what would happen if they were to be found by Mbuya Mandiopera in her fields."

Everyone knew how important it was to make sure there were not in those fields. Mandiopera was a hell raiser. The others would be bowling over in laughter. On the ground, his Auntie would now be. She liked to tumble on the ground whilst having a great laugh and it would fuel more laughter around. Uncle Kenneth still wanted to fight, but Rhayi would simply pour water on the fight with his usual statement of taunt and triumph.

"Apo bhoo nemastatement pahuro. Ndabva ndakudzipa." Meaning, literary, "There, I have hit you with facts on your neck. Now I have strangled you."

Uncle Kenneth would simply have to join this laughing choir, he would start by chuckling, and then he would hit the stride with his alto-cum-tenor voice, even Uncle Patrick, who was slumbering in his hut would add his huge bass voice, laughing himself crazy. He literary howled every other voice off the arena with his bass voice. After all, everyone knew Rhayi was going to play this hard ball, that way.

***** ***** *****

Mandiopera was a very tricky customer. If your cattle stray into her fields, she had a way to deal with you. Other people would come over with the cattle to your place and insult or shout you down, yet others would take the cattle to your fields and let them graze your crops whilst you were watching, doing an eye for eye act on you, yet others would go to the Village Headman and report it as a crime. You would be tried by the village and payment was imposed and extracted from you, to pay for that. It

53

would be in the form of 50kgs bags of whatever crop you have denied these people of harvesting.

Mandiopera dealt with this differently. She would come over into the homesteads and let rip off you; shouting, scolding, insulting, calling everyone names in this household; even the dogs, cats, trees, houses are scolded and given names. It would be like being slammed by a very huge wind, a tornado, and in its calmer part- the eye part of it- she would strip naked, completely naked. Then she would tell the men of this household to come and fuck her. She would point it, where they should come and fuck her. The men knew of this and they would run off the moment they see her coming with the cattle and hide until she has left. It was shameful, a painfully shameful thing. It would make you feel so bad with yourself, that you have caused or invoked such an old lady's anger up to the extent of striping herself naked with anger.

Yet, there was another Uncle, his father's half-brother who once got into this fix with Mandiopera. Mandiopera came and did her thing. She shouted and shouted until she reached the point; she stripped herself and told Uncle Vincent to come and fuck her. Uncle Vincent was a hot hire. He took it up his ways. When he couldn't stand it anymore, he hit the roof with anger. Uncle Vincent just broke the nearby tree, took a big stick, and beat the naked Mandiopera on her buttocks, raging, and shouting, as well.

"Kupenga kupengai, kana munhu uchida kuripwa, taurai mhani," meaning, "Angry, what's this kind of anger. If you want me to compensate you, say how much you want, hey." Beating Mandiopera, until Mandiopera realised she was being beaten. Out of her angry tornado, she picked up her clothes and run off, as she would try to put her clothes on, also avoiding this uncle's sticks. Uncle Vincent chasing off Mandiopera with a stick was a story everyone always enjoyed retelling...

***** ***** *****

AND THESE WERE THEIR REASONS

She would be telling us a story of her life, growing up in the Handina Village in Rukweza, Rusape. She would sometimes sing a song that reminded her of those days of her youth.

The axe's handle has fallen down the mountain
Give me advice, Father
The axe's handle has fallen down the mountain
You are the earth, Father
The axe's handle has fallen down the mountain
Suffering is stubborn, suffering is stubborn
The axe's handle has fallen down the mountain
Give me advice, Father ...

She is so emotional and, then she breaks down crying. We cry too, and we don't know why we are crying; only that Momma is crying.

It sometimes is a simple story about how they woke up very early in the morning to plough in the summer, or ferry the firewood from the mountains in the winter season with her brother, Uncle Sheppard. Sometimes, the story becomes difficult and hard to take when she talks of how her brother had his eye destroyed whilst they were ploughing; saying a small stone, or a piece of wood swung out of the soil and hit him on the eye, thereby cracking it. That, they thought it hadn't done that much damage, so they didn't make him visit the hospital in time. When it became too painful, that's when they took him to the hospital.

56

When they visited the hospital it had become so bad that the doctors couldn't fix it, so he developed a bad eye that couldn't see.

For years, growing up, I was scared of Uncle Sheppard. He seemed to be staring at you as if he was seeing you but he wouldn't be seeing you. Then, he would twist his face a bit so that he could see you with his only eye that's still functioning, and the dead eye shines through you. Hearing this story always made us sad, angry with life; that it had caused such a thing to happen to our Uncle.

Sometimes we were made to hate our Grandfather, my mother's father, and the step granny, for bringing that trouble upon his family. Momma sometimes says it is this second wife of his father who had caused that through witchcraft and, that she wanted their family not to prosper. Sometimes she would say even the death of her mother was caused by this step granny. It only made us realise how having two wives was a bad thing to have on your family, but we were young to really understand it all, so we sometimes thought Momma was just being too emotional.

Most of the times, we will ask her to tell us those stories of growing up, especially the funny stories of her mischief. We would laugh crazy as she tells us of how Momma and her friend, Louisa Magocha, would come into the church late when everyone was sited. They would be wearing South African clothes her father sends where he worked, and everyone in the church is so shocked. Momma will tell us they will be wearing skimpy fluffiest tops, boots, feather tops, dangling earrings and short skirts. Laughing, giggling, like silly girls, in the church; and behaving like

57

utter freaks. Sometimes they would wear a cheap, sweet bubbly perfume that would reel the little boys to them like doting doves. It was obvious Momma was such a beauty in her teenage years. She still looked beautiful when she was telling those stories. But, it is this anti-rules attitude and behaviour; that was so controversial, especially doing that in the rural areas of Rusape that would have us taken, surprised, even shocked and we would laugh with her. And then, when she had sobered a bit she would start on the difficult stories. Sometimes we will tell her to stop it. We didn't want to be sad, but sometimes it just comes in, a story like that, sad; without our having figured out that, yet. She always gets the better of us when she starts some of these stories the way grandmother; our father's mother started her own stories. Grandmother Helen told fable stories and, that way it was easier for mother to fool us that she was about to tell a fable. In which, later, she would divert into those sad stories. And so, she would start, and we would have to listen…

"This story happened under the conditions of prejudice, uncertainty, resentment and anger. Some few days before the story happened had seen disagreements, fights, and just that unreasonable want to enter into battle; between the people on one side, and the animals on the other side. The day before, a black Mamba snake had killed a young boy herding goats and, this fuelled the people's anger and in revenge they waged a full-scale hunt for this snake and killed it."

And then, the little boy of this fable; she would tell us later, was a local boy of their Rusape Area and that it really happened.

Yet, we thought we were listening to a fable. But, in the meanwhile, she would continue with her fable story...

There were the three of them; the animals. The Chameleon, The Gecko, and The Frog. To a meeting with the people, and in order to discuss on how they were going to live together peacefully, the animals sent these representatives. To diffuse such a dangerous situation, a meeting between people and animals was called. The animals sent relatively peaceful representatives. Thus therefore The Chameleon, The Gecko and The Frog were sent as representatives to the meeting.

We would question Momma how humans could talk to animals. It was impossible to our young minds. It still isn't possible for people to talk to animals? Would you tell a Black Mamba snake to stop biting what it doesn't even eat? There is this special breed of the Black Mamba snake that we were all so scared of, and it is known as Rovambira, the dark brownish black puff-udder. Mom told us it is the most dangerous snake you can ever come face to face with because it is such a fiery fighter and very poisonous. Mom once got into a face to face situation with it. She was up in the mountain, Muzamhindo Mountain. She told us; it was after that boy in the fable like story met his own death through being bitten by the poisonous black mamba snake. Though we knew she was just mixing these stories to derive better impact, of her own story, we would still listen amazed. When she combined those different stories we sometimes thought she could beat Grandma Helen any day at storytelling. She would continue with her fable story of the animals.

In order to appease the animals' anger, arrangements in favour of the animals' representatives to this meeting were made by the people. The meeting was held outside the village, near a pool of water. A good shrubby tree and a light-grey glinting hard granite rock gently dipping into the water made it both beautiful and spectacular. It was also an assuring and peaceful sight to behold, so that the meeting proceeded, decisions were made, and a commitment to enforce them was made. So, it seemed a successful meeting.

After taking a heavy breath and, thinking through her thoughts Momma would come in with a totally-crazy-to-our-young-mind, statement. She would say; a meeting can only be successful if its solutions are followed through to the end, when implementing it, to the benefit of the society or a country. We are wondering what society she is talking of, or the country. She has just been telling a story or fable of snakes, or of animals. So, what is this new thing she is throwing in, we ask ourselves and, or sometimes we ask her. In doing that, we would create a break in the storytelling. She would take some time to think through her answers, and then she would push our minds further, challenging us, saying that listening is the biggest part of storytelling, of any meeting, too. That, one has to listen very closely what someone is saying in a story, or what people are discussing on, or even agreeing to, so that one can be able to communicate that further on. She would later tell us we have to listen to the story, and ask questions later. Sometimes we will fight her, telling her that when she finishes the story we would have forgotten some of the questions. We want to ask the questions before she finishes telling it. But, like grandmother would do, she would threaten to stop telling the story altogether if we won't listen to her. Of course, we will stop haggling with her and listen to her story.

For some seconds or minutes it is as if she doesn't want to continue. We are so scared she is going to stop altogether. She is so quiet, she is staring into the fire, she is in this world of her own and we do not even exist in her world. We feel so left out, sometimes we cry silently because she is also crying silently as she watches the flames of the fire. After some time she heaves a heavy breath, and in a small quiet voice as of a little girl she continues...

She reverts to her story of the snake.

She says the day she climbs Muzamhindo Mountain, a dangerous mountain, she is looking for the sour kind of wild berries that she likes known as *Matunduru*. She isn't even close to the tree when she sees the wild rabbits scaring away. She is thinking it is because they have seen her that they are scaring. So, she proceeds to the tree, anyway. She hasn't climbed the tree that further up when she starts smelling this funny smell. It is the smell of cooked sadza of grounded rapoko flour. She looks around thinking, at first, there is someone who has left this sadza nearby or is eating it. When she doesn't find anything, she knows what this means. She knows it is somewhere, near her, so she jumps from the tree without even trying to check where it is. She strains her leg in the process but is up before she knows it, and she is running down the mountain shouting, crying, and hallooing in a high girlish voice for the people in the village to come to her rescue. She feels it behind her, sliding in, swooping in, and coming for the kill, hard on her heels. But that, when she could

61

snap a glance at her back, all that she could see were the hard silhouettes of Muzamhindo Mountain, curved against the sky.

The whole village, sleeping in the sun, is awoken from its afternoon slumber, hearing her calls, her cries. The strong man of the village are preparing and getting into battle mood, some are already running towards her cries, and Uncle Sheppard too, without anything to fight this monster with. They are calling her to keep running especially upwards the terrain, or in a stone path, or gravel or sand path where its progress would be hampered. She listens to their advice and takes a sandy path. She creates a bit of distance between her and this Rovambira snake. But, it doesn't let go that easy once you have disturbed it at its den. Worse still, once you have defrauded it of its food, the rabbits it was about to kill, which you disturbed by intruding upon. It wants your blood, come-what-may. When it is this angry it comes into the village, bite as much as it could before it is killed. The smell of a dog, and their village is with a lot of them, even makes it a lot angrier. The snake's smell makes the dogs bark and whine recklessly in fear. So, the village has arranged itself into battle lines waiting, yet some have already forged into battle. They want to close off its retreating ranks when the battle come full-on. They know, once my mother has come into the village, with the snake behind her, the battle lines will close in on the snake, so that it won't retreat back through its hind ranks.

My mother runs, and she tells us she runs and runs, and she can't even collapse, yet... She knows she isn't safe. All she could see ahead of her were the mud coloured huts blending in with the brown grey of winter landscape and trees. Behind her, the monster snake is still near even though it has been slowed by the

62

stones and sands of the little pathways. It is still bearing down on her. Momma keeps running and running, and all she can hear, in the middle of her laboured heavy breaths, are people's voices calling her name, whistling, hallooing her to come down near the river, into the river's sands.

And then, Momma would just leave that story hanging and start talking of the fable story. We are so angry with her for leaving us that hung up but we can't protest anymore for we do not want to invoke her anger or tears. We know this fable has been included to make her cool off, or just to work the story around to the conclusion. Grandmother Helen did this differently. In the middle of the telling, grandma would say.

"Jonathan Muzukuru, please go out and fetch some firewood. The fire is dying."

And, I would protest strongly against this, because I am afraid of encountering one of those Zombie baboons, or killing hyenas of her stories. It is dark, dark night of the tropics. It is a dark that talks, whistles, sometimes screams with sounds that can cut you into pieces.

"Grandma, I am so scared to go outside. There are Zombie baboons out there", and I would lie to substantiate my fear, "I have heard one of those Zombie baboons crying, just now, now, grandma, please, please...."

She would laugh that off, saying she isn't telling the story if the fire dies. Then, I have to create a ball of strength within me to confront the monsters outside, or lose the story altogether. So, after waiting a bit thinking that Momma is going to reverse back to the snake story, we have to take it on the chin by listening to

63

this fable we don't know what it really means. We simply have to listen. She is continuing with the fable, anyway...

When those representatives, The Frog, The Chameleon and The Gecko returned home they called for a meeting to let every other animal into the outcome of the meeting with people. To this meeting, and from every kind of an animal, a representative is asked to attend. All representatives are there at a jiffy. When they have grouped together thus the onus is now on those three representatives but to emphasise it all the more, the Hare thus enforces.

"We now want to hear what transpired at the meeting with the people."

But, none of the three volunteers anything out, maybe they are feeling out of depth to come forward and explain everything, especially to such a group that comprises some of the cleverest animals like The Hair, The Leopard, and The Lion. Yet, they are not to get out of it that easy. The Hair isn't allowing them such pleasures.

"If none of you is willing to start on it then we will have to make our pick..., suppose we start with the Frog?"

The Hare declares and every other animal nods in approval.

"Now this is unfair." The Frog thinks to himself.

"Surely it's unfair..., it's very, very unfair. Why would I always get picked on..., why me? Why had the Hare left off starting it out with The Chameleon or The Gecko? Could this be because they enjoy my songs? It could have been easier to copy, with different words though, what the other animals could have said."

But, he has no way out other than owning up to the situation.
64

"Maybe they will enjoy my singing. I really have talent here....uhuu...ya-aha, that tune....yah."

In his sweetest tones the Frog thus sings himself out of the situation.

"We went to the meeting
But there was nothing,
Nothing that I heard
I love singing
I love singing
I love singing

Look at the Gecko...
Oh the Gecko...
Dancing to my song
Look at the Leopard...
Oh the Leopard...
Whistling to my song
Look at the Hare...
Oh the Hare...
Singing to my song
I love singing.
I love singing
I love singing

That's what I was doing
Singing at the meeting
I heard nothing

65

That's what I am doing
Singing to you all
I remember nothing
I love singing
I love singing
I love singing..."

We are now singing with momma to the song. We love the songs, especially when she isn't singing an emotional song. She is a great singer. She sings like a bird trilling in the trees, uncaring of anything, other than its songs. In the beautiful girl's soprano voice, she is so carefree. We are so into the singing. We are clapping hands, whistling. We are enchanted.

"Look at the Lion!
Oh the Lion..."

So, the song goes on and on and in short the Frog is saying.

"I am sure all of you know that singing is what I am good at. I suppose since The Gecko was always banging his head, sometimes so harder on the granite stone, he must have heard and understood quite a lot about that meeting. I won't waste anymore of your time now but will rather call forward The Gecko".

In the heat of enjoying and dancing to the Frog's song, The Gecko is taken aback when The Frog stops singing. We are taken aback as Momma stops singing, as well. We don't know what would come after that. We are like those animals in the story. Our eyes are now focused on Momma's face with hunger for the story. We want to know everything at once. We want to get into

66

her mind, her soul and wrench the story from her but we know we have to hear it from her, to listen to her story, to wait for her.

All the other animals' eyes are now focused on The Gecko with murder in mind. He really has to deliver or else he will be killed by the other animals. The Gecko knew that was coming. He knew it. He knew that the frog was going to pass the buck. Being the lame duck that he has always been this was coming.

"Why can't The Frog stop singing, at least once when important things are being discussed? Just see what his singing has caused..., talent be damned, surely not at someone's expense, no!" The Gecko mutters to himself.

We are asking the same questions of our mother. Why did she have to stop in the middle of the song? We would have wanted her to continue singing... It was such a great song.

The Gecko has to say just something, at least anything to soften the animals' anger. At least he has one irrational; often frustrating element to his nature that can be his wild card to rescue.

"I didn't hear much about that meeting..." And so, The Gecko starts and stops.

"See the dark anger in The Leopard eyes, the cold calculating mischief on The Hare's face and The Lion can hardly stop himself. Sorry, sorry friends, I know you are angry with me. I know I have to be punished but let me meet out the punishment myself..."

The Gecko starts banging his head on the granite stone, even sometimes a lot harder if he feels they want him to do that, and then starts talking again.

67

Us, we are thinking; The Gecko must have taught our Momma this trick that well- that is- diversion. Momma has done that to us several times. We are afraid of questioning her. Sometimes, when she is not telling the story and we are talking of something else not very important we would tease her, telling her that she is always like The Gecko in the story- that is- she always diverts a lot. We tell her she would do that more than even Grandma Helen did in her stories. She would laugh that off and tell us we are too young to really understand. That, in life, in making decisions, people always divert from their course and takes an easier route. Even in a meeting, people have a tendency of diverting from taking a difficult decision, by creating a world or a solution they want that would make them feel good with themselves. She would throw in the fact that even in the country's governance; politicians have that tendency, as well. She would throw us off with that statement, of course! We didn't know one thing about the politicians so that was always too deep with us. When she has thrown us off she would say even The Gecko was throwing everyone off in the story and, was avoiding the reality of his life, time and his failure to have listened well during the meeting with the people by blaming The Frog; saying.

"It was because of The Frog who was always singing beautiful songs which made my listening and understanding the issues discussed very, very difficult. Ok, it's not a good enough reason but you really have to understand what The Frog's voice can do to someone listening to it. Ok, ok, ok, please don't..., please don't, don't kill me, please, please.... Let me bang my head a lot harder this time."

And so, he starts banging his head again, a lot harder this time such that one can hear the paw-paw sound he is making. When The Gecko feels the animal's anger has been sated, a little, he continues with his speech. Whenever he thinks they are angry with him, then he reverts back into banging his head on the stone. This is the speech he gives in between.

"My ears were listening to The Frog's singing; my eyes were watching The Chameleon who was always changing into beautiful, different colours of everything that was happening there. It was such a beautiful sight and that's why I had to bang my head. Sometimes really that harder like what I am doing right now... I was thanking The Chameleon' efforts at photocopying the information, just look at the beauty The Chameleon is capable of... Just look at that!" Momma would continue, branching into the snake story...

"And, it is the smell of a snake that gets The Chameleon so worked up and into a violent behaviour. When it is angry or when it is under threat it runs as fast as any snake you can think of, children. The two don't stay in the same place, ever!"

Momma tells us this as she reverts back to her story of the snake, telling us it is The Chameleon that saves her that day, and save the whole village from dealing with several of the puff udder's angry bites. As my mother is nearing the river where all the other people are waiting for the battle to consume the place, this snake tries to cut the distance between it and my mother by swooping through, on top of a green shabby, thorns infested Musosawafa Tree, and fails to scale it properly. This tree, the-cover-of-the-dead (Musosawafa) tree, doesn't only protect the graves from being opened up by the wild dogs. It stops the snake

69

in its spiky thorns and in so doing; it disturbs The Chameleon in its slumber in this tree. When something does that to The Chameleon, especially sandwiching it painfully against a thorn, then The Chameleon can only do one thing it is capable of. It gulps a good part of the middle part of this Rovambira snake in its wire-cutter-like, mouth. Once The Chameleon has gripped anything, it has gripped for the life of it. So, The Chameleon does that to the snake and the snake tries to bite The Chameleon off its body, but the snake's poison doesn't affect The Chameleon, in any way, at all. Once a snake is bitten or wounded, especially by its middle body, it becomes weak. It is easy for the people to kill it without a sweat, thanks to The Chameleon.

After killing the snake, the people's eyes were now on The Chameleon. It is an animal, so it has to die. Despite the fact that it had saved them a calamity, they kill it. It is even a lot easy because it is locked into the snake's flesh for the life of it. Momma then hits a parallel, to the animal's story, trying, I suppose, to make us believe it is the same chameleon that saved her. Giving it a lot of room in getting out of its duty of that moment..., which was to have listened well?

Maybe, it is an act of guilty with Momma, that the villagers killed The Chameleon that saved her. But anyway, she continues with the fable story...

All the animals' eyes were already focused on The Chameleon who had already started his displays. When The Chameleon knows that every eye is now focused on him, he starts walking very slowly.., so slowly, in his undecided, slow way to the front. On the way The Chameleon entertains with his rare quality of changing from one colour into another. Through all that he puts every animal into an expecting suspense. At least every animal is now hopeful because the treat they are being subjected to now was just a bonus.

"Iiths-s-s was-sh-ss- aa-a sush a-aa color- Lar, fu-ful, beaut-ti-uti-tiful-lulu shpect-acu-cular-ar occa-sshi-shion." The words coming out syntactically jumbled, he stops, and then in his broken, undecided, slow way he continues.

"And, for the first time in my life, I was too busy, so much busier than I have ever been. There were so many, so many things to record..., the wisterias were there too, you know I love the wisterias, such beauty... hu-u..u.."

He stops again. This time and for a long time, in the meanwhile he changes his colouring to match that of The Lion, The Leopard and The snake. Even its long time enemy, The Snake, is enjoying it and can't run away. Every animal is amazed. Not even the Hare can force The Chameleon to continue. At length, at his own time he continues.

"I thank you all for giving me such an opportunity to witness, record and enjoy such a spectacle..., but... But I...but I don't remember anything that I saw and heard that day. I had to always change from one colour into another such that by the end of that meeting I had forgotten everything that I recorded..."

"It was such a hectic affair but I only hoped that The Frog and The Gecko could still remember..."

"Shii...shii...shii...shii. Thee-ee-ezi... no no nee-nee-e-ed for you-u-u to-to ge-e-et ma-e-ed izi the-ere...?"

71

The snake hits the grass, running as fast as it could. The Snake knows it didn't want to be at the mouth of The Chameleon's anger.

"What the heck is this all about anyway?"

Was that Momma saying that? This time she is not crying, maybe…. Maybe, it's a question we ask mother, sometimes. I suppose it's the question every animal is asking each other. It might really be The Chameleon who has found his strengths, running and talking as fast as is possible, off the meeting…

And so, that was that, Sadza rekuBoarding! You eat it whether you want to or not. There is no other alternative.

And, these were their reasons.

FINDING A WAY HOME

He remembers him, his brother Mutimutema. He was his beloved older brother. He can still touch it with his breath, how he loves him. He still loves him; he knows he can blow the float for him. They were born the two of them in their family, by an ailing father who couldn't hold longer before he returned back to the ocean cradle of birth, to see his only two boys growing up. Their father died when they were barely 10 and 12 years old respectively. His brother took it the harder way; he would speak of it, when he was younger, his speech sometimes breaking into a cry song, baffled why things had turned that way for them. Mutimutema had always been the serious of the two, but his father's death cut him into two.

Mutimutema had since started being trained to take over the throne by the ailing father. Their father, King Chitsakatsaka, of Chitsakatsaka Kingdom, it was a kingdom that was made up of Buhera, Marange and Chipinge Areas of the present day Zimbabwe. So when their father died, the king's regent, an uncle, continued training the brothers, especially Mutimutema who was the heir to the throne. The regent was a kind and affable man, and ruled the kingdom well on their behalf. But Mutimutema had other ideas.

73

He didn't want the throne. It was a curse, it had taken his father. Eventually he had worked things out of his system long enough to get at fifteen, a developed young man. But, he still felt his brother; Hatsakatsa, had every right to the throne, just as he had the right to it. He loved his brother and he didn't understand why only one of them had to get the throne. He felt it shouldn't be him, so he created the beginning of the end of all that. He never told anyone he felt that way, though. He never told Hatsakatsa of his plans. He built them, quietly to himself. As he hit his fifteenth birthday, and he knew the next year, on his sixteenth birthday, he would be enthroned the king, he left home. By then he was a revered fighter and hunter and he knew he could survive the forests, so he left, northerly. He didn't know where he was going. He was the compass finger, mindless of its past, directing himself on this dangerous journey. He was lonely, but he knew he wasn't unloved, just alone. He knew he would grow stronger and sad in this journey. He only knew to be the king of Chitsakatsaka Kingdom was not his calling. And that was the last his family and brother Hatsakatsa saw of him, but they heard through passed-down word that Mutimutema had passed through other kingdoms to the north, that he was herded to the north.

They tried to send parties to look for him without success, and then he disappeared completely as he was swallowed northerly. That was the last they heard of him. Now, King Hatsakatsa wanted to think Mutimutema was successful. Hatsakatsa, on his sixteenth birthday, was enthroned the king of Chitsakatsaka Kingdom which he ruled well. He was well loved by his subjects and the king's tribune and household. He was a

74

very good leader. He bore the throne three sons and three daughters, and now, 60 years down the line he was old. His throne was secure.

He was now seventy years old, and all through this long way here, he never forgot his brother Mutimutema, what had become of him. He remembers when they were young, and they would call each other in the darkening forests. Now their lives were knitted in those forests, their voices calling out to each other in the dark. He had named his first son Mutimutema, and this young Mutimutema reminded him more often of his brother. The likeness was unbelievable.

When Hatsakatsa was alone, every night, at his king's abode, he would ask himself, he would question himself about his brother, especially as the time his brother disappeared approached. The same weight of the past and future had aged him. The feelings were too much for him in the first few years, but now, it was memories that he cherished. His life, rather than an excursion into unfamiliar places like Mutimutema's life, had been an adventure, a journey. The journey was a condensed image of his life, like making offerings, votive offerings to an unknown god. He had been thinking of his brother, for a couple of days, and tonight he was alone, by the hearth, in the kings' Dare (an outside home where the king would carry out meetings and socialise), when his major-domo disturbed him.

It was a rule that he should not be disturbed when he was alone in this Dare, and the King knew it was important that his major-domo was disturbing him. He allowed his major-domo to proceed with his message. Word had come through the villages north that a certain King Mutimutema, of a kingdom to the north, in the present day Kenya, had sent word to King Hatsakatsa. To explain the significance of such a message to Hatsakatsa, at that moment, when he was engrossed in this subject, would involve going into great details. The message was this: King Mutimutema was dying, and he wanted King Hatsakatsa to send four of his best hunters or warriors up north, to help him secure his kingdom against another malevolent king who coveted his throne.

King Hatsakatsa knew that was his brother. He knew, that night, what had become of his brother. For the first time he felt unsure of himself, of what he thought he had achieved in his life. He felt how too sure he had been with himself, for a lifetime of it, how he had thought, and would feel he was connected to things. How he had felt his house was secure, had been built for eternity. How he had been attempted to believe in stability, which on one hand hardly took the effects of growing old into account, and on the other hand made every external change look like a catastrophe. He had forgotten it was an ongoing process. He knew he had forgotten this so as not to succumb to fear, for fear makes our minds snap shut to ourselves. It cuts us from ourselves. His brother sprouting from the dead, the un-living to the living prompted all the more these feelings. He knew his brother was letting him know he was alive, and that he had done well for himself, and that he still loved him. He knew his brother was dying, and he wanted his family to take over where he was leaving. He wanted something, someone familiar to leave his legacy with. King Hatsakatsa knew he couldn't make the journey himself, he was too old for such a journey. He knew what he was going to do to show the same love to his lost brother.

76

The following morning he called a meeting with his subjects. In this morning the meeting continued as the King said to his subjects.

"I have gathered you all here today to help me decide a very important matter. There is a king; to the north who sent word that he wants me to send four very brave men to help him secure his kingdom, so I would like you to help me, you are my people; to select for me these four men."

One of his subjects asked him.

"What kind of men are you looking for, your royal highness?" King Hatsakatsa replied him.

"I am looking for men who have distinguished themselves as warriors and hunters, but still young, still uncommitted, men who are looking for a little adventure...like my son here, Mutimutema." Deep down his bones, dancing deep down his marrow, he knew it wasn't just an adventure; this journey would change the travellers. He knew that travel, which seemed to be a light dream, a seductive game, a way of freeing oneself, was merciless.

Everyone gasped with the mention of the King's oldest son, the heir apparent. Mutimutema was thirty, and very much ready to take over from his old father, any day, and they were surprised why the king was doing that to his son, even when they knew he loved his son. Some thought the king was just making an example, by the mention of Mutimutema's name, but the king offered, even a lot more,

"My son, Mutimutema, as you are all aware of, was named after my gallant brother Mutimutema, has proven to you that he

77

is capable, so I want him to be one of these four men I will be sending."

"But he is your heir to the throne, my King."

Mutimutema's mother questioned, full of motherly concern over his son, whom his father was sending to the wolves without care, but Mutimutema put everything to rest as he strode past all so all things would pass.

"Yes, I would be honoured to be one of those four men. I will make you all proud of me. Thank you, your highness."

Even though a lot of people still felt it was uncalled for, they accepted the young man's decision. It was now a song of his heart he had chosen to listen to, a faraway song floating, in the notes of music of the leaves, the voice in the leaves as the wind played them. He was the son of the king, heir to the throne, he was a king himself. He knew what was right for him. The choice of the other four went smoother, in fact, all those who were chosen felt honoured. It was the song that had surrounded them, their faces were the music, so eager; and the pace of the sound was now their heart. They had to play their song not listening, as if they were nobodies, as if they were not even the sound. They had to play their songs not with their hands, not with their eyes, not with their eyes, but as if it were with their hearts. These included Shamirai, Chimutsa and Nyere. Four young men, very brave, intelligent and courageous, there were four of the King's best young warriors and hunters.

The King gave them a day to sort out their private matters, a day he knew he wanted to make a goodbye to his son. He knew it was going to be permanent. He wanted to make it last, and it was a debt he had to pay that way. The four had to also be

78

strengthened by the spirit medium of the place, so that they could face the journey with courage. The King also knew these four men wanted some time with their loved ones, especially their girlfriends, whom they were making a last farewell to, without knowing it. He knew it will be a last surprise to these girls. Offered like a farewell present to a departing guest, as a token of love.

After the lapse of that day, the four entered into their journey. They were very eager, like little kids given all the freedom to do whatever they wanted to do, without adult countervailing authority. Every traveller into an unknown territory does not have a very developed sense of reality-for the tangible facts of his journey. These four thought they could do this journey inside some couple of months, or a year at most, return and take over their lives, and enjoy telling the stories of this adventure to their girlfriends, the community, and later on, to their kids. It was a dream excursion for them. Travellers do not always manage to distinguish dreams and reality, and often confuse dreams which surfaces in the form of colours, scents, and sudden associations, with the strange and secret convictions of a previous life that reality is, in which time and space do not separate them, anymore than does the light sleep of early morning separates a person from night and day, thus what they call reality is what they can grasp with their own hands, and what concerns them directly, which to these four travellers was to deliver their message. But when travelling the reality's appearance changes with the mountains, trees, rivers, stones, air, the way the earth was arranged, language, and the colour of people's skin. These four were blind to all that, theirs was an adventure, a small adventure into the known unknown. Somehow they thought they knew what they were going to face, the way a child seem to know things, but as the child grows older he gets more confused and confused, until even at old age, he was more confused than when he was in the teens.

Their plan was they would walk into the next kingdom to the north where the message had come from, and get told which next kingdom to go to, until eventually they had arrived at the kingdom where the original message was issued. That's how news travelled then. Time then was a net of feelings that would across into the unknown with a sense of confidence or daring, with anticipation or with dread. Yet those four were chasing the message and time with a filigree of hopes and expectations, knots of joy and relief; that they were going to achieve on what time would take a lifetime to import through. They were going to do it inside a year, at most, they thought. They were too sure of themselves, that sooner, their journey would be completed.

So, they would ask the king of the place they reach whether he knew of the King Hatsakatsa, and of what message the king had sent through to King Hatsakatsa.

On the first day they travelled through pristine forest, they saw abundant fauna and flora as they headed north into the next kingdom, of King Mupeta. They knew that's where they could get an idea of the next kingdom to visit, where the message had last came from. It was after over a week's travel that saw them arriving, by the dusk, into King Mupeta's household. That night they slept at the king's home, were welcome as the two kings, Hatsakatsa and Mupeta, were long time good friends and had helped each other in defending their kingdoms in the past. They

80

were still closer to home, the home they knew. When you are still closer to home you don't ask yourself a lot of questions, you just revere in it.

Before the sun was up, the following morning, those four travellers left on their journey into the next kingdom where the message was said to have come from. They begin to realise that theirs was going to be a long journey, as they trundled through rough, mountainous terrain, waded through deep rivers, and steep slopes. They were leaving home as morning closed its eyes on them. And it was this day that started their toughening up. Late in this day, deep into the afternoon as their legs started complaining, they came to this very large river, a lake on the move. Like Save River, would look when it was flooded. They didn't know its name but it was too deep and dangerous. They supposed it was the Sambesi (now known as Zambezi) River they had known from folklore stories.

And, as they tried to contemplate on what to do, they entered into their first fierce argument. Mutimutema wanted them to take their time and build a boat, a small wooden craft to help them cross the river, Shamirai concurred with Mutimutema as he said,

"Yes, we could take a week or so to build some craft to help us cross this river safely, plus we would cross unharmed. There are bound to be crocodiles in this river. I can feel it in my bones that we could get into trouble, real trouble, if we become reckless, as Nyere is saying."

Nyere, a colossus' sized young man, hit back as he said:

"Shamirai, are you afraid of crocodiles you are not even seeing. We can help each other if we get attacked. They can't be

81

many of them here. We have the armoury so it won't be a problem. Gentleman, we are the bravest men around all the kingdoms here, so let's not waste time by creating this woman's dress you want us to wear. We don't need the boat." Nyere, he was always in a state of great stretch, like a bow that was just waiting for the moment when the arrow would shoot towards the sky.

Chimutsa, always a bit on the soft, unless he is confronted with danger, also supported Nyere, even though deep down, his bones cried out against him. Generally, he was not begging or demanding, he was not expecting or even waiting, he was always so completely in the present, that nothing else existed for him, but now he knew, it was a dangerous excursion. Even for him to come all this way, in this journey, he had to disdain the voices inside him, telling him it was a wrong cause for him. But, he had had enough of this living in a cage; he was not satisfied with his life that bordered on dreams, intuition... He wanted to be raw strong, like Nyere, or a strong and thinker like Mutimutema, or even playfully strong and inquisitive like old gossip, that Shamirai was.

He also knew of that terrible dream he had had the night he was chosen for the journey. In that dream he saw a huge monster lion that was chasing after him. He was almost about to be torn by the lion's fangs when he exploded in this night; crying and waking out of the dream, with tears actually rolling off his cheeks. He had known that night it was a futile cause for him, but he knew he couldn't excuse himself over a dream. There was a force, insane, deep down his soul, pushing him, telling him it was fate, which he had to face. He knew his time to face to his existence on earth had come and he was prepared for it, so he took Nyere's side. The two fighters fought from their corner, fiercely; the two were very good orators, as well. Eventually they convinced Mutimutema and Shamirai they could save a lot of days by finding a shallower crossing point on this river, and get across it that same day, unharmed.

The four started checking the river, northwards, and eventually, and it was almost night's fall when they came to a shallower crossing point of this river. They looked at it squarely. It was about a hundred metres wide, and they knew they could swim through it, and the river wasn't that dark green at this point. So it meant it wasn't too deep. So they started swimming through, unconcerned what might lie in this river. They had buried their fears behind their minds' back. In a skyline now a bit dull and lead-coloured, of the sunset's, it took them a moment before they realised they had made their first mistake. They saw two water holes whirling towards them from the banks across where they were herded towards. The crocs usually bask in the late afternoon suns on the banks of a sandy shoal, and since these two crocs had heard game in their river, they had entered it quietly for food. When the crocs are basking in the sun, they burrow a bit under the sand such that it was a few who would discern them on the beach, but they would hear any sound, every sound close by, in or out of the river. They had started approaching those four humans unnoticed, until some five meters or so, when the humans realised their mistake. The pair of crocs knew they had fair game as they circled the four who were now huddled together with their spears drawn out, but powerless in a river strong and deeper than their feet could reach the bottom.

One of the crocs made a lounge for Chimutsa's left leg, trailing a little behind, as the other croc fooled Nyere into thinking it was diving for him. In a splint second, fear touched Chimutsa, an ugly stain on his being. Are these the lion monsters of his dreams? Chimutsa howled in pain and Nyere drew his sword towards the croc that had duped him, jibing the water, fiercely.

It took Mutimutema and Shamirai a bit longer to come to Chimutsa's help as they were also duped with Nyere and, were a bit ahead of Chimutsa. So, by the time they came to grab Chimutsa's hands, the crocs had each got a good grip of Chimutsa's two legs and were dragging him to their rock cave to the south, where they had their home there. The four fought harder and organised themselves. The four's conditions of existence, they knew would not now be haggled over or negotiated for with these crocs that would simply gut them, crash them, now at a moment's notice. Nyere made a strike of one of the crocs, by its middle part and, it bellowed in pain, as it let go of Chimutsa's other leg. The humans dragged Chimutsa and overpowered the other croc, but it didn't let go.

As they approached the sandy banks the croc, seeing that it was losing out, hooked water into its tail and held onto Chimutsa. The three people couldn't pull Chimutsa, as they realised what the croc had done. They knew if they pulled him anymore, his leg would be torn into flipping pieces, so Mutimutema told Nyere and Shamirai to keep holding Chimutsa. He swarm back into the river, underneath the water and found his way to the water knot the croc had created with its hooked tail, and beat it by the tail, very hard. It let go off the water knot, it let go off Chimutsa's leg

84

and swarm back into the river, to nurse its injuries in the cave where the other croc had since retired. The three travellers made it to the banks. Chimutsa's legs were gushing streams of blood, but they couldn't wait to fix him.

They didn't rest on the banks; they knew it was suicidal to do that.

They carried Chimutsa off the banks of this river and in doing so they made another fatal error. Chimutsa's legs were dripping blood all the way to this resting place, thus he lost a lot more blood, and by the time they stemmed the flow of blood, he had lost a lot of blood, and was very weak. In the confusing trees, some of which had leaves still green, some had taken on the autumn yellowing colour, some had fallen, perched were crows: evil, triangular, their eyes.

The three looked around for food, wild fruits to give to Chimutsa, which helped him a bit as his condition became stable, but he was still weak from loss of blood.

That night the four slept on the ground, but on different places, so that one of them could at least survive, if they were to be attacked. As per their mission, they had to forego having to sleep close to each other, in order to make sure someone would survive to deliver the message. They also slept on the grounds rather than up in the trees because they knew Chimutsa couldn't climb the tree and, they had to be close by to protect him. Downside of this, it had its own weaknesses. When you sleep on the ground and when you eventually fall asleep on the ground, your body would get used to the ground, it would be a deep sleep. On Chimutsa's side, as the muti medicine used to treat his legs started being effective and exclamation marks disappeared

85

from his face, he fell into a swoon sleep. He closed his eyes for the last time.

By those early hours of the morning, when the four had entered into a deep sleep, those two crocs had by then dealt with their pain. It was now a numbing pain, and also deep down their guts, the hunger wrecked them. To top it all, the human blood they had tasted made them wild with want of human flesh. So, they came out of their cave, out of the river, onto the banks. On the banks they followed, using their very strong sense of smell, the blood of Chimutsa. They were now courteous hunters because overland they had a lot of disadvantages against humans. They stealthily followed the blood spots and smell, off the river's banks. Instantly they knew they were closer to the humans when the smell of humans was strong. Stealthily they made it to where Chimutsa was in deep slumber.

One croc gulped Chimutsa by the throat, gutting its teeth into his voice box such that Chimutsa didn't make any noise. The other croc gutted him by the middle and the two crocs held Chimutsa off the grounds as they dragged him to the river. Chimutsa couldn't fight them anymore for he was weak from the loss of blood. It was easy for these crocs. The other three humans couldn't hear anything for they were in deep sleep, and a bit away from Chimutsa.

When the three woke up, they were surprised to see that Chimutsa was not there anymore. They courteously followed the new blood spots and the treads the crocs had created back to the river, knowing full well what had happened.

When they arrived at the river banks, all sight gathered on what was on the sandy banks. They were confronted with the bones, hairs, scalp and blood on the banks, and knew they were of Chimutsa's. They knew they had to leave the place. They knew they had to run off; that they didn't even have to collect Chimutsa's left-overs for burial. An anguished fullness raising from the waters- the restless, boisterous water- and the sky above infinity itself, motionless, told them it was suicidal to stay any longer. They left off, in a hurry, and ran as far off the river as was possible. When they knew they were now safe they started walking. They couldn't talk or even try to accuse each other of this folly. They knew the enormity of their journey now. The home they had known, the way to this home was indivisible. They knew the more they had travelled away from that home, the more they would now have to travel, a lot too far from it, for them to find their way home again. They knew they couldn't go back, so they settled on their journey. Tears were now useless waters and they had no time for them.

They walked that day, ate very little, drank water and walked some more like possessed things until way after night's fall. At night they climbed a straight tall strong branched tree, tied themselves to those branches, using strong tree bucks and fell asleep in this bedroom of theirs. They didn't sleep that night, they were possessed. They couldn't talk that day; they were autistic, clump, dump... They did this for two weeks; walking, eating very little, drinking a lot of water, slept little, talked little, still possessed by that wild thing they didn't know its name.

It was a feeling of pervasive emptiness, in their heads and stomachs, their legs almost breaking; cracking and their feet tearing off. But they nursed those legs and continued on their journey northwards. After these 14 days, when they were

87

beginning to talk, they entered a semi-desert land. The crushing heat in this semi-desert land seemed to echo a harmony of shapes and colours, the horizons becoming bigger and emptier, the wind stronger and hotter. They welcomed this baking, this stifling heat, they welcomed this cooking. Here and there, were sand dunes, melancholy, familiar; their presence in a former lifetime, in dreams and memories of past years. The burning earth, the burning wind- constant and relentless- the sight of the mountains in the distance, desert vultures drifting in silence, black, some white, some grey; flying away with a light beating of wings, ominous.

On another day, slowly as the semi-desert gave home to more trees and grass, they crossed a river and entered into a very deep dark forest, more immense, the horizons close, more threatening. The forest stretched out in front of them, an impenetrable darkness beneath a sky almost as black. They could barely see where they were going for it was thickly forested. In a little after they entered this forest, it got misty and their sight became even a lot short.

As it got darker they suddenly found themselves surrounded by three lions. It was a family of one cub, one male, one female- the mother of this cub. By all measure they were ready to pounce at them. Instantly the three companions hugged a tree, circling it by their backsides. They looked, stared hard at the lions. Those humans seem to have turned into something else inhuman, to these lions. The lions were now afraid of pouncing at something, or some human form that was static, had six pair of eyes, and was staring at them. They were stopped right in their tracks, and they stared at these human forms that had turned into statures.

88

The male lion tried to frighten the three by roaring in its blustery huge voice, changing from its relaxed and unfocused energy and becoming tense and agitated, as if primed for an attack, but the three remained put, even when everything around them was shaking due to the roars of this lion. They knew it was a matter of survival now. The male lion even tried to attack them but they stayed put, and it stopped, right near them. They hadn't flinched.

Throughout that afternoon the lions kept vigil, waiting for any wrong move, and as it grew darker with night's fall, it started raining heavily but the three travellers stayed put, so did the three animals. When it was pitching black, the three travellers imitated, at just the same time, the huge bellows of elephants. They knew how to do it convincingly. It's something they grew up practising, but they also had the help of the noise of the slashing rains. The lions and elephants don't share the same forest or habitat, just like two kings couldn't share a kingdom, peacefully. So, the lions abandoned their place in a hurry. They didn't want to have to fight with the giant over this place.

This had freed the three travellers and they eventually found a tree they could share; tied themselves up for the night, and slept in. Later that night, a pale moon sailed above them, apologising for coming out late, a frail thing.

In the morning they continued with their journey northwards, passed hallowed out human habitations that had survived the test of time. And as they left this forest, they could see, tucked into the hallow of a hill, a small village, fields, cattle, and other husbandry. They left this now thinning forest by midday, and as they came into the heart of this kingdom, they realised the line marking the border of this kingdom, it seemed, had shifted backwards to those hallowed out human habitations before. So, they eventually found the King's place and relayed their message, only to be told they hadn't arrived at their destination. The journey still had to be accomplished but in the meantime they rested. It was now deep summer so they decided they needed to take a break from the summer's rains, flooded rivers and rainy season's diseases. They also wanted to eat healthier food, to strengthen their bodies for the forthcoming journey the following autumn.

They were given some piece of land to cultivate by the King. They were also offered wives, by the people of this kingdom but refused to take these offers. They knew they still had the journey to complete. They ploughed their patch of land, became part of this kingdom, and by all means they enjoyed their break. The crops did well and as they started harvesting their crops, Shamirai started finding his calling. The playfully, inquisitive and funny Shamirai went to play. He thought, as usual he was playing, just a little bit, but later he discovered things had shifted for him. The way simple things in life have the ability to affect us in ways we never imagined, or thought they could do to us. The earth, which is always in perpetual movement, is bound to affect us. We are affected by its ebb and flow. By its oceans, plates, seasons, air; without even realising it is happening. We are affected by everything that happened even in lands so far away from our visible or tangible environment. Usually we forget all this just to keep the peace of our souls, which are built on shifting sands. What we thought as the right thing to do, all along, becomes so wrong, as we find ourselves.

All through the summer Shamirai had made friends with an old blind lady who had been deformed by leprosy. The more he got to spent time with this lady; the more he helped her, the more he got closer. His calling came, and took place during that summer.

This woman stayed by the outskirts of this kingdom, abandoned there by the community because people of this area accused her of being a witch. Some people couldn't even stand her sight, and a lot of people couldn't stand the sight of this old woman's granddaughter. She was the most beautiful person in the whole kingdom, but everyone thought she was cursed. They said she was this witch's companion.

This old lady had had a family of twelve children, including the father of this granddaughter, all of whom, including their own children, had perished through the leprosy. This granddaughter and the badly damaged old lady were the only ones spared, of those affected by it in the entire kingdom. It killed a lot of people of this kingdom and those it maimed were later abandoned across the river, away from others, in which they all died. This old lady had survived after this granddaughter decided, against the whole Kingdom's displeasure and dissuading, to live with this old lady across the river, in this leprosy colony.

This granddaughter had nursed this old lady for over two years. The old lady eventually fought her way to life, but she had been badly damaged. She had to be carried around by the granddaughter, for everything, even for ablution needs. Her hands and legs were some small pieces, deformed, burned-out logs. The granddaughter took the old lady back to the community and tried to claim their land back, but was told by the King that it

91

was now the king's land. She was also told she had to build their home outside the kingdom, so that when the disease comes back again, she wouldn't have to affect others. These two had built outside this kingdom.

Their former land was now the land the three travellers were given by the King to farm that year. This is how Shamirai started getting involved in the life of this old lady. He felt they had taken what rightfully belonged to the old lady and he felt he had to pay off this guilty feeling he had by helping this old lady and the granddaughter.

They had a small patch outside the kingdom, and Shamirai, that summer, helped the granddaughter in preparing it and cropping it. As he spent a lot of time with these two people he became attached to the granddaughter. He felt he wanted to protect her, to help her reclaim her rightful place in the eyes of the society. Before long they were spending a lot of time together, as lovers. Shamirai felt right to be with her. He felt he had arrived home. The leprosy episode had happened in this far away kingdom to his Chitsakatsaka Kingdom way before Shamirai and his companions took this journey, but its effects now affected him, seductively embracing him in choosing a destiny for him. It was not a hunter's quarry for love. It was the peace of his soul, to be with these people. It was freedom's precious gift to be able to get in touch with his home. He embraced it, heartily. So that as autumn came through the two travellers, Nyere and Mutimutema, failed to prise Shamirai off this place, as they left on their northerly journey. Shamirai had since moved in with the old lady and the granddaughter. He had given his hand in marriage to this granddaughter.

92

The two travellers continued with their journey, knowing full well that they had to reach their destinations. They had to find their way home. It was no longer about getting the message to the King, in that far away country, but it was now about trying to find their way home. Before the death of Chimutsa, their journey had been about to deliver the message. Now it was different. Chimutsa's death had changed the matrix. His death was a school only too likely to teach them of life's inevitability, of meetings and separations arranged haphazardly. What was a fleeting image only a moment ago, a brief halt, had now become an episode, a slice of life. Each of the three left now knew they had to find their true worth, their true homes, deep inside them, and Shamirai had done that. He had done that in the past summer that had come to an end, and now, the two were part of the journey again. It was now left to the two, Nyere and Mutimutema, the reality of yesterday, in the sadness of their departure.

The two travelled for days on end, ate whatever they could find in the forests, and travelled some more. In this journey, the reality of the day before yesterday was an event from a bygone age, which would never come back again. As those days made weeks, and weeks made months, and months piled up, the two kept on their trail. What had happened over those past few months of their travels now belonged to the realms of dreams and to a former life?

In slightly over six months, they found their way into another kingdom. It was a kingdom in the grip of a war, with another kingdom to the east. The unfolding of a life is made up of nothing more than a finite number of such episodes as wars,

93

death, travel, eating, living, or even just being there. So, into war, they had entered. They were absorbed into it. These two, in their Chitsakatsaka Kingdom had been the King's two best fighters, so it was a blessing for the king to receive such awesome fighters. He knew some day they might leave, so he involved them in the leadership of the war effort, in order to entangle them. In no time, the two were spearheading the war effort.

They waged the war successfully, and pushed the usurper from the east back eastwards. Two years later they overwhelmed this kingdom, took ransom back to their adopted kingdom, and were revered, praised and the gifts mounted. The King, very pleased with these two fighters, offered them his daughters. He had only two daughters and he offered them these two daughters, and a claim at the kingship.

He also offered them the best places to farm, hunt, and keep. He offered them co-leadership of his army. And he also offered to give them anything they might want. He even told them they could complete their journey and return back, and claim all these offers. At first, the two took to these offers, after they had discussed it between themselves. It's inconceivable for someone to spent over two years in one place, get involved into its affairs, become part of it, and just dismiss it. If we don't spent the rest of our lives in that place, chance alone will be responsible, it could be anywhere, it could be somewhere else, and it doesn't really matter what the place is like.

In all his life, Nyere felt that the place where he was going to finally build his home would depend on a thousand chance possibilities. He was a fighter. He just lived life with an open palm, viscerally. He knew he would come to a place, to a point in

94

his life where he felt he had to just give himself up to it, whether what he was would amount to anything or not. He only wanted to give, to fight for his breath, for his existence. He had fought a war he had enjoyed. He felt in that war effort he had fallen in love with this place. Whatever it now offered him wasn't very important, but what he felt he could continuously give to it. It would just happen, and he felt it had happened. His journey had already happened, it was now a finely cut grass, soft and thick, in his memory, one that had been woven hour by hour, day by day, year by year from his breath, sweat and blood, and irretrievably lost, for time had worn seven league boots since they had been on this journey.

But the night they took to these offers, Mutimutema had a strange dream. In the dream, he heard the voice, his voice calling his name, "Mutimutema", "Mutimutema", "Mutimutema", and he would answer, "I am here", "I am here", "I am here", and follow the voice. It called him, out of this kingdom, and he followed it. He found himself in another journey, again. It was to the north. It got difficult for him, in the dream, to reconcile himself from the Mutimutema who was on this journey, to the Mutimutema who had been on the journey, all the way from the south. This Mutimutema who was now on this journey was older, even though he knew in his younger self; he had been alike to this older version of him.

In this split personality, he began to realise that he was no longer alone in this embodiment, for his namesake was now a part of his body. The older Mutimutema, his father's older brother, he realised was alive, somewhere in the north, and he had to find him. It was no longer about delivering the message;

95

somehow he knew that message had something to do with finding Mutimutema, the old one. His father, he realised in this dream, had known where he was sending these four men. He was paying a debt, and every debt is paid in full. He realises he was that gift, the two doors of gold, that had been wrapped in very fine paper- the fourteen doors of silver- in the form of his friends; Nyere, Chimutsa, and Shamirai. Now the gift was on the open. He was alone. He understood his mission. It was a subconscious coming to this understanding, though consciously, when he woke up from this dream, he felt something had been playing a trick on his consciousness. The dream couldn't really have happened, so he disdained it.

That day he got married, in a double ceremony with Nyere, to the King's daughters, and his wife was the youngest, and the most beautiful in this kingdom. In that night of his wedding, he met his wife on bed for the first time. For the first time, in all his life, he crossed the bridge. He had always shied away from crossing this bridge. He was transported into a world he had never even imagined, even in his dreams, by the pure chaste love of this king's daughter. For the first time in his life he found himself in the maddening heights of love making, travelling into his inside. He knew there was a stone inside him he had to melt, and he allowed himself to travel toward it.

He found it, he surrounded it, he tried to nibble at it, and he tried to break it apart with this passionate lovemaking. He achieved orgasm, he hit the roof, but deep down he knew, in the aftermaths of this passion, that he had failed to melt the stone. He hadn't found his feet... He knew that stone was the voice he had followed the previous night, in the dream. He knew he

96

couldn't defy it any longer. He knew for him to become complete, he had to melt it, and that it wouldn't happen through loving this daughter of the king, or through any wealth offer, or through the kingship, but through finding his path on his journey. He had to reach his destination; he had to deliver the message of his father, to complete the circle that had been started, way before he was born. He was the last arc to join up that circle.

In that night, when his new wife was in the deep sleep, the happy sleep of blissful love, Mutimutema took his armoury, a few food things, and entered into his journey again. He started on another trek to the north, now on his inner journey to find the stone, to take to the voice inside him. He left everything, everything that could have made sense to anyone, everything that had made sense to Nyere. He left his seed, which he knew he had planted in the king's daughter, in order to find the voice, to melt the stone. He gave himself up. He knew his child, someday, would want to know what drove any man, this man, to leave such bliss. He hoped, someday, his son would come to understand that some things are out of our grasp, out of our will, out of our want.

One only has to follow the voice inside him; one has to dance to the promptings of his voice. One has no power to refuse, to resist. One simply gets swept in a cauldron, of this movement, this impetus, and it is a fate. A fate Mutimutema, knew of the following morning as he found himself, over ten kilometres to the north of this kingdom. He was chasing this fate. A fate he knew was going to change him in ways he never thought of, or even imagined. The man who had left the king's daughter was different from the man who left Chitsakatsaka Kingdom, over

97

five years before this moment. He knew he was broken in his un-brokenness, but he also knew it wasn't enough.

It was another half a decade when Mutimutema was still walking. He didn't know whether it was walking he was doing. Maybe it was an act of survival. He had survived, he remembered, those days he had been rained down, down to the bone-marrow. The skies, clouds heavy skies lowering themselves abruptly like a heavy canopy intent on suffocating every living thing beneath it. He had survived the day he had fallen down in an avalanche of soil, stones into the lake, nursing his broken leg and finding himself out of this lake of his existence. He supposes; it was in the southern parts of the great lakes region of Africa.

He left the lakes as he climbed the mother of all the mountains. He couldn't avoid it like all the other mountains he had been able to avoid. It stretched beyond sight, east and west and he knew; it might take him far away from his compass if he were to follow it, whichever direction, until he reached where it ended. From deep below it, the mountain was a beautiful blue white capped dome, with indentations on it where huge rivers flowed down into the lake below. It was a sleeping huge elephant, contained and totally motionless within its skin as if its whole self had been compressed and thickened, such was the quality of its concentration. The path he created up this mountain sloped steeply upwards in long looping curves, sometimes in narrow sweeping hairpin bends. But he tried to avoid tackling it straightforward, which he knew could have broken him.

The clouds were covering its top like plumes of smoke, adoring this high place in misty adoration, but he knew on top of this mountain he might die from coldness, so he took with him, as he climbed this mountain, dry logs of wood to ignite a fire. He knew a mountain was a living thing, climate infernal, he had to first consult with it; by studying it, its feelings, its desires, whether it was obscured by the clouds like it was, or held in sunlight, before he climbed it. The mountain is a reservoir that has collected so much that's come from the sky, like snow, ice, sprouting springs, etc..., so that if one consults its feelings well, one could bath in its sky-high energy. He took his time in climbing it up, checking what was happening on top of it.

As he got closer and closer to its top, and it was after several weeks of climbing and resting, it got clearer and clearer. He knew he had done his job well; he was going to be part of the mountain's inside environment. Like this mountain, he didn't fear anything, he knew he could now absorb anything. He feared nothing, not even his own death. That night, he found some cave on top of this mountain. It was a cleft rock cave, where he bedded for the night. He ignited a fire, and slept, cold down to his marrow, but he survived that night. The mountain was clear of the clouds and rain, and the ice was melting. It was melting off him, and he was lucky it had started melting when he had reached its summit or else he would have been submerged in its flow offs, if he were still on its slopes.

He ate some fruits and started walking on its top. He began to realise how mountains were living things that defy any other living thing that might took habitation on its body. He bathed in this sky-high energy as he walked on its summit, and below it, looked hazy. Even though walking was still killing him, even though he was so tired from his journey up this mountain, he was

99

grateful to it for its generosity, that it freely had shared this atmosphere with him, for it was a gift, this high-up feeling, that could not be experienced anywhere else. Deep down he knew it's not the mountain he had conquered. No, it was him he had conquered. He was no longer afraid. He knew the only things that climbers or even travellers conquer were something inside them. Their fears, their doubts, the impossibility and limitations of their existence! To complete a journey, or to climb a mountain, he thought as he walked down this mountain, as the mountain sloped slowly downward, gently into the environment, is to come into the journey's presence, or even the mountain's presence, to be within its incredible atmosphere. He knew he could now make the journey.

He had also dealt with a pack of hungry lions that had chased him into a straight tall tree. He was lucky he had a good headway with this pack or else he was going to be their food. For a day he had stayed put in this tree, and then, he remembered what else those monsters were afraid of.

He developed and threaded a very long string from the trees' small brushes and tree-buck fibres. When the slumbering lions below were waiting for their prey, Mutimutema had thrown, pointedly, that string on the biggest lion in this pack. The lion thought it was a snake that had fallen from the tree, that was about to bite it, so it heaved and roared off in fear, and run off this place. The other lions knew what it meant. The lions are afraid of snakes, so the pack disappeared in a huff, off their prey and Mutimutema alighted from the tree, knowing that those beasts wouldn't return back. He walked a bit of some distance in

100

this night, and found another tree to sleep-in. The following morning he continued with his journey.

He had also survived a band of savages of the Manguru tribe hell-bent on eating him, telling them that he was a cursed person, behaving like some mad spirit in search of a home. Using signs he told them they had to leave him alone, or else they would bring the bad spirits on themselves. They couldn't eat him, so they chased him off their tuff.

Five years since he had abandoned his newly wedded wife, and everything that had some semblance of connection with where he had come from, and it was pitching dark, of early winter evening when Nyere was still walking?

This day he knew he couldn't stop walking and pitch up camp in the trees as he would do days before. In his bones, he feels he has to continue walking. In him, there is this sense he is chasing a light, a wispy of luminosity. He can barely raise his legs but he can't stop altogether. Sometimes he would stop for a moment, and then remembers he has to make another footing, off his feet. He would try and he would do it, and the walking would continue.

He is climbing a cliff, off a river he has just crossed. He is rounded in extreme exhaustion. He knows with icy certainty that now it is creeping upon him, dulling his senses, slowing his movements, all the time urging him to fold down. But he can't stop. He is seeing some light; it is far off the highland, off this cliff. He can barely breathe, but still he soldiers on, and on... In him, he knows he has to reach this light. It is the light he has been chasing, in his dreams, for the past five years. It is the light he has been chasing all his life. He is now 40 years old, what

101

importance do these numbers have, or timetables, he doesn't know; only he knows he has come Full Square to sad manhood, chasing this light. He knows it was only due to a series of chance encounters, events; fortunate ones in his view, that he was able to pass through all those kingdoms, and come all this way.

He knows it is now downhill for him from this moment onwards, but he is still climbing the cliff. He can't stand anymore. It is still whispering to him to just fall down and lie quietly, and be done with it all. How could he dare this nightmare territory gnawing away at what is left of his consciousness. His eyelids droops and he sighs deeply as he falls on his face, in a huge heap. For some time everything goes blank for him. When he comes back to consciousness he understands what he has been attempting to do. He has been attempting to move, but his muscles are locked. He massages his feet, his calf, his knees, and he relax a bit, but he can't still rise from his feet. He is so weak, so he starts grovelling on the twos, then threes, and then fours, sometimes on his stomach like a snake. Time stops as he grovels off, it has no price tag attached to it, it is a dead thing.

He keeps on it and can't just give up. He knows he has to find that light, he has to reach it. Then, deeper into his slumber, he hears the barking of dogs, and he knows he is closer and closer to humans, to a home. He feels the dog's smell in his nose, but he can't stop grovelling on his feet. He keeps on it, as he hears people being led by these dogs, to where he was. He has since collapsed but, in his mind, he has lied to himself that he is grovelling. It is an act of survival. His mind couldn't give up on him, and then everything goes completely blank.

Two days later find him still walking. He has been walking, in the pitch-dark world he had entered. The light has been playing hide and seek with him, but he didn't want to give up. At one moment, he sees it and he strives for it, and another moment, he sees only pitch black. He is stumbling blind in this darkness, but he can't stop. He is still moving, walking... He is still fighting, on his knees, grovelling. He still wants to reach his destination. He is still following the prompts of the voice, now softer, sometimes so sweet- a woman's voice. It is deeply embedded inside him, in his consciousness, pulling him in. He feels the stone inside him melting, and he is not doing anything, as such, to make it melt. It is just happening. He is breaking through a very dark forest. He is still walking, walking and walking. He takes a huge breath, pushes himself, pushes his legs, pushes his frame, pushes and pushes and pushes, and then it breaks. He hears the crash, in the form of a voice. He says, as if in a voice deeper inside him, he is asking himself a question.

"Mutimutema!"

Someone who is walking into the hut smiles at him. She is this strikingly beautiful girl who is carrying a gourd of porridge. It smells heavenly. It is a fine winter morning, with the sun's warmth penetrating into the insides of the hut he is in. The early light, bringing with it all the blurred and shifting memories of the past dreams- the sunlight is soft- with a soft silvery intensity. The fire, which had warmed him throughout the night, was now dying off. It is the smile of this woman that warms him, down to the cockles of his heart.

She starts spooning porridge and feeding him. He wants to ask her why she is feeding him. He looks into her eyes and she

103

smiles the answer to him. He eats, but his eyes don't leave this woman's eyes. Was he still dreaming? No, everything is now normal. He can even feel his legs and hands warming up from the food, from the smiles of this sweet lady. Was he still walking? No, he had arrived. This woman was his destination. She is the one he had anticipated, all his life, with obsessive patience. He had arrived at his home. In between gulps of porridge, he says again.

"Mutimutema."

The woman smiles again, and nods her head and then says in a language he had last heard over five years before, when he left Nyere behind:

"Yes, Mutimutema is the king of this kingdom. He is my father."

He rises up from his sleeping position. She tries to stop him, but he brushes her away. Was he the king? Was he this Mutimutema? No, he remembers of that dream in which he had dreamt of an old Mutimutema, taking over his being. Has he done that again? He touches himself, he realises he is still his old self. Then everything starts connecting, making sense to him. It's his father's brother who is the king of this place. This is where he had been sent by his father. That's why he knew he had reached his destination. The old and new had been connected, the circle had been completed.

He has to find this Mutimutema, to relay the message from his brother. He takes this woman's hand, and urges her off her sitting position. He knows she is part of the circle. She is his hand. That's why he has taken her hand, without any doubts. She leads him to her father. She knows where he wants to go.

Her father is in a deep slumber of a painful sleep, so they wait for him. The shadows in this hut are stark and lie across the walls. Forming long angles, like claims to a life, what we feel it owes us, that goes back so far that memory itself is stretched, and has not gathered the necessary forces to wrangle with words, preferring this long and sweet and dark complicity. He is dying, Mutimutema realises this hint of truth, trying to tell it, there is no mind, no words, as he also realises how much he looks like his father, like him, only frail. His hand is still in his woman's hand, and he looks at her. She smiles at him, with understanding. Then he realises, why.

She looks exactly like his grandmother, his father's mother, Mbuya Natsai. He instantly knows what her name is. He knows it. They wait silently for King Mutimutema to wake up from his slumber for nearly half an hour. When the king woke up in a gaggle of coughs and blood, they help him into a sitting position. All through this process, his eyes were locked into the young man he has found with his own daughter. He knows who that young man is.

He had received the message in the dream that he had had when those two were waiting for him to wake up. His time was up, a voice had told him. It was now a complete cycle. In a gaggle of coughs and blood he started telling this young man what had happened, in another lifetime, back when he was a young lad. He talked a bit about his journey to the north, but he didn't delve much into the details, for he knew this young man knew just as much.

"When I arrived here, over 60 years ago, I helped the king to the north fight a very bitter war with the king to the west. I fought bravely for years on end and the king was killed in that battle. Everyone begged me to take over the throne but I declined, so that his younger brother took over. But I couldn't decline marrying the king's daughter who is the mother of Natsai, you are holding her hand." He stops a bit as he takes a good breathe, then continues.

"As recompense, my now new father-in-law, the king's younger brother, gave me a part of his kingdom, this southern part, as my own kingdom. I became the king of this area and we have lived peacefully with my in-laws. Her mother couldn't survive her pregnancy, to see her blooming into the beautiful flower, my girl is." He gaggles and coughs for a very long time, and they help him as best as they can. Eventually, when he is breathing normal again, as he continues.

"Now, I am dying. I know who you are my son; you are my young brother's son. There is no mistaking the similarity. I knew you were coming, and I knew you would make it. I waited and waited. I refused to make a pact with death, I just couldn't die. I fought death every day, for over 10 years it took you to reach here, waiting for you. Now I can go. I have made my pact with death. I have connected with where I came from. I have seen love from my family, through your coming here, and making it. I love my brother, just as much as he loves me. This is my only daughter. She is the diamond I have held in my arms, in my being, all of her life. Now, I am going, son. I want you to take care of her. I want you to take care of each other. I want you to make each other happy, and that's all that I want my children. Thank you for making it all possible for me. You are my spirit, and I am now going home."

106

He blinks; double blinks, gasps a bit and closes off. His body let go as he relaxes, slacking, and his eyes become static. The two knew the king was gone. They knew what to do. But they had to wait until they had buried the king, to really complete the circle, to start creating their own home.

OLD MAN, DREAMS, WRITING

We had had some words with the old man, in the afternoons. He stays in Felicia Street, number 9,

and I stay in Douglas Road, number 9, so our places are opposite

each other, opposing each other like polar points, dissonance, like synchrony

It's an upper middle class suburb; Birchleigh North, in Kempton Park, Johannesburg.

This old man I am writing about, in my dreams, is a prickle old thing, complaining at the slightest raise of any volume. He sits on his veranda that overlooks our backyard, where we are supposed to play, but we can't make noise. Its midday, and he has tea, a big cup, clay cup and a plate of biscuits, I think, store bought ones...and he is happy. A beam of sunlight hits the top of his bald head, like a penlight flicking on. I am writing; I stare at what I have written about him. Did I show you, so far, that I don't like him? I am not saying I don't like him. But, I am writing

that I don't like him. Are they the same? Let me check the page. I stare at

the page , at most precisely, the space an inch to the left of my ball

point pen, an Eversharp pen- looking for a word, a phrase, a

thought, that is trying to jump out of the sentences,

that is trying to make you have sympathy on this old man

108

Some things don't just change...I have been using an Eversharp pen

for over thirty years, since my grade school, and there was a Bic pen. Bic died,

did it, and Eversharp stayed Eversharp and I am still using an Eversharp pen. And if I am

ever sharp I can prod spatial pleasure from the texture, textiness of this text, whilst the intellect

in you is confounded. I gaze as if these words might feel my gaze, like a slight breeze, and behave well. I want this writing to be the rope I will follow from this dark forest slip of dreams, in these severe and

relentless thunderstones, to the Ellesey Suburb, so that I might feed with all the others there.

I want the old man to behave, as well. But would you tell someone that old to do that

Not him. Unless if you want to write it, his answers, a column of ten...soldiers

arranged for an invasion, battle of Normandy for you

.... you!

.... you!
.... you!

..... you!

.... you!

.... you!
.... you!

.... you!

.... you!

109

.... you!

.... you, and he will continue calling you, ... you.
You would almost think, it's now your name, as he goes inside
to the phone, to call the police. I stayed
with my brother at this place,
so he was having a party for his little kid who
had turned 1, and he had invited
his friends over. I didn't know how others were
doing but I, personally, I was getting tanked.
It was George, his vulgar friend who matched this old man.
Replying every of his .... you with an equally fucked up .... you
of his own. And the whole party crowd joined in, calling the old
man, ... you, ... you, old faggot .... you, everything became ....
you, the party was .... you, Douglas Road became .... you,
Birchleigh north .... you, I never really liked the place. It was too
white. We were the only black
family in that street. And fucking enclosed with
electrified barricades, and only one gate
out of it. If you wanted to go to two streets down us,
which was outside the barricades,
you would have to go up 8 streets to the exit point, and
then take Straydom Road,
down 11 streets to Pangolin drive, which is just two streets
from Douglas Road
The place was an island, curved out for the protection of one
race. The
neighbours, who were white, also entered in, calling us .... you

110

The police came and called everyone at the party, …. you. This situation was feeding backwards and forwards, running ahead of myself, and then rolling

off this pen. Like the barking of dogs, I have just gone out of our gate, and suddenly;

it is dogs, dogs, dogs, as I go up to the gates. Black hair, of mine, spiking up like stalactites

It's the noise of dogs barking, wanting to eat me. It's the Whiteman's dogs that are the vessels of

the white man's dislike of a black person; even black dogs don't like my colour. But they are black, like me. I see a white guy coming up ahead of me, and there is silence his side of the road, and when I pass him, the side of the road I have left is now silent, and his, which I now plod in, is dogs, dogs, dogs. Like these dogs, the policemen, mostly black policemen, took everyone at the party to the

police station. We fucked up in the police cells that night. We had to bribe them off,

for them to let us the …. out of the cells. The old man didn't get out

of his house for a fucking long time, though. Scarred like shit

he became fucking polite afterwards, sometimes joining

us in our fucking noise. We dealt with a lot of fucking curses from

our neighbours. We fucking didn't care. It's supposed to be a fucking

111

free country. Oh! It's because I had taken my sight off from the writing that I have been swearing, to stare at the clouds outside the window, to the north, around

Ellesey Park, just off Pangolin River, just off Pangolin road, just off this place I liked. It coloured

Well. The clouds looks like burnt clay, were besieging the black, burnt out walls of the northern sky's fringes, as if the clouds were descending to rebuild this sky. I had been watching that sky, hardly noticing the swear words I had been writing, hardly noticing the change of light around me, as night was becoming morning. I think to look at my words again. It is a superhuman effort to make my eyes focus on the pen again. It is a dream hare on quicksilver feet, the way

       my pen is creating mountains and conquering them in its writings,

       creating oceans and swimming across shark infested oceans,

       typhoons, hurricanes, tsunamis…all that. I look again at the sky, where

    they might have been this view; lost space, lost words, long into the woods

And then, the face of that old man slipped back through the window I had forgotten to unlock when I was watching the northern skies, and he tells me, or possibly, I think he tells

me, that, it was him, that old man who lives at the house across ours. I know that! That was the old man who was waiting for his beard, purplish whitish as a branch of rowanberries, to grow down into the ground, and root himself to the dead. I tell him that…or he tells me that. Someone must have told him that in

112

the fight, that night of partying. My gaze focuses on the words I
have just written. It never
      strays from the spot at which the pen has just moved
away, the complete line finished,
            the stanza, perhaps a poem. Although the old man
was as solitary as a finger,
                  a dream deep inside him warmed him. His head
is a skull; one could see
                        the shapes of the bones. I want to know
his name. I ask him
                  what his name was, is. He keeps silent,
but he is looking
            at me with a look that is a name, which is his
name. I see it in
            his eyes, and I know it is in my eyes, too. With my
hand still holding
      the pen, I stain to hear the old man. My pen is firmly on
the paper, on this
   page, the old man's voice is in the sound and smell of the
pen's ink, the scratchy
sounds the pen is making as it scribbles the paper, like whispers
on paper, like sheet music,
like a ghost. He is dead; it's actually his skull I am seeing. He has
been dead for two years now, he tells
   me. I had left Kempton Park 5 years ago for another city in
Johannesburg, Germinston, and later for home
      That's where I am home, in Chitungwiza, writing about
this old man. And, I had been thinking he was still alive, but no.
He has been dead for over two years
   113

I ask him where his families are. He tells me he was the only son,

his parents were long since dead when I met him, and he had

never married. My mind agrees with him. All the months

I stayed in Douglas Road, I never saw anyone,

family; coming to see him. Then, I thought, he just didn't

go with crowds, but now I realise the truth. I ask him again what

his name was. I hear my voice in his replies. He answers me in my own voice

He is me. A strange chain of associations sweeps me into a crowded maze of recollections,

and then, prompted by a faded memory lodged in there, leads me to an irresistible curiosity, but then, my words sets me free… maybe it's my writing, that's less clear to you, a handwriting of the

Eversharp pen, not my thoughts. Or, I must be undecipherable, me, Hildegard? He is me in

these trenches of my schizophonic (not schizophrenic) mind. I am staring at the sharp

serrated stones of my life's story.

I wail!

I howl!

114

A voice of blue that shoos the clouds,

I mourn!

I cry!

How nice to notice myself amid this half-conscious offer!

I take my skull which is on his shoulders, and put it on the head

that was not mine. It fits in like a self container (inner self) that springs on this

page, and then I am walking off... I don't know where to. The morning star hangs over the

Birchleigh north area, like a drop of blood, giving out so much darkness, yet producing startling light. I am going to the home of an elderly lady who was my first girlfriend, who had hurt me those long, long years ago. I reach Glenmarias Cemetery at the hour of witches, three AM. Every wave of the wind,

an ally, I find her place on the soil, the land mounded (by death's carnival ride) and ragged,

undirected, voluptuous strict. In the trees, the sitter-hum of night birds formations.

A bird flies overhead, between the mangy crescent moon, and my left cheek.

I hug her mound, I cry out the waters. She now lies on this ground,

stripped into the ground, into the soil, unraveling sutures,

as lonely as I am now.

115

DEAR LIFE, DEAR DEATH...

Life

I want to write to Life? I couldn't find the address to write to Life; neither did I know whom else to write this letter to, that's why the letter doesn't even have a physical address. In my darkest moments, before I had muscled courage to decide to write to Life, I asked around where Life lived.

"Where can I find you Life, do you have an address?" Life then laughed at me, he cackled in sardonic humour.

"Are you crazy? I don't have an address. Maybe you should write to Jamaal. I am in you, Jamaal, remember that! That's the only way you might reach me." Life replied me, and I couldn't help asking myself how I could write to myself. How could I hear myself? I needed someone to hear me out, so I came to an understanding that Life was doing that usual thing, deflecting things off of his body. Because, between Life and Death, the two should know to whom this letter called. So, anyway, I decided to write to Life.

Some time ago, I was dealt a heavy hand. I know I would rest only when I have played all my hands out. I was twenty five, Jamaal Mukonomushava is my name and, I have been such a wreck for some time. My life has been a mess. It got messed up; it is now almost three years ago. I was born with this heavy hand; I was born in a family of an apostolic sect, Johanne Africa Apostolic Church. My father and my grandfather were of this sect, so I had to be of this sect. In my little village of Chibvuri,

116

my people, the Mukonomushava people, the bulk of, were of this sect. It was as simple as that! The only problem was we were not allowed to access medicines, or even a hospital when we were ill. Which was another heavy hand?

"I could only use my pen to play my hands." It's the point I am getting at in this letter.

"Like that adage that the hammer only knows one thing?" Life enthused loudly. Striking the nail in and, everything else is a nail to a hammer, that's what life is trying to say to me.

I only hope that Life gets this letter. I needed to write this letter because there is something that's been a terrible torture in my heart and mind. It means, all these three years I have just existed, and people can exist in all sorts of levels. Breathing is not even the base for existence. I have existed this way; breathing, tortured peripatetic breathing, all over the landscape kind of existence. It's now either I have to say it out loud or continue being weighed down by its corrosive hurts until God knows when? So, I start with the seemingly premeditated conversation with Life...

"Life..., you know that, not so long ago, she was here with me." And, he replied to me, funnily enough, agreeing with me as if he really meant it.

"I haven't forgotten?"

"What haven't you forgotten, Life?" I couldn't ask Life that question, though. I needed to be sure we were on the same page, so I asked him about Dora, again.

"Have you forgotten her sweet chastity and warmth, Life?"

"I haven't forgotten. How could I?"

117

I see Dora again in a vision, it's a broad daylight vision I am having. She is sited under the baobab tree, in a floral creamy dress, light brownish pushovers, that gives some sense of gentle contrast to the fields. Unladylike, she is straddling on top of the huge baobab tree's root, eating the baobab fruits. Dora is a sweet girl. I had known that; that she was a beautiful girl, and for years, I have been lacking in courage to talk to her, but this day I find the courage as I sit beside her and talk to her. I am thinking of this day as I ask Life.

"Then, how could you do that if you haven't forgotten her, Life. Why would you do that? What you did was cruel, Life?" I am not actually saying this aloud. Out aloud, I could only ask him another premeditated question, again. I still wanted to know, why?

"Have you forgotten the true light she shed on my otherwise darkened life; the faithful and trusty shield that I leaned on in my times of troubles, Life?"

Those were the things that I liked…, loved a lot in her, more than anything else; they were the things I could have had, if I had to choose. Back then, I didn't have to choose. As if it was written in the stars, we were there for the other straight away. In no time we were in love. The next moment we were married. I was very happy as she got pregnant with our first tries. It was always happy times to be with her all through her pregnancy. Without preamble the nine months of the pregnancy period came to pass but the child refused to leave her body. She became huge and huge like an elephant as the baby girl overstayed inside her body.

118

"I know you are going to talk about her body, her face? I haven't forgotten that too, fool?" Life intruded into my musings. Such cruelty was in his reply!

"Bastard!" I exploded. I couldn't help exploding, and then I continued, now softened a bit by this explosion.

"I want to talk of her sensitivity, her inspiring and understanding help, her hopeful disposition, as newer and truer as the spring's sprouting lovely greens!" I softened a little bit more as I continued, "Her form, her face, those are just fleeting things, Life. So, I won't obsess about them. It's her true nature I have alluded to above that matters to me, Life and, It's you Life who used to let me have all that."

"No, it's not me." He blatantly disagrees with me. "It's you who would have them, Jamaal. It's you who lost them."

"It's you, Life..., you betrayed me!" I pushed it all the more.

"No, it's Death who betrayed you." He deflects pressure off of him, again. "You should have taken her to the hospital in time, not to believe that nonsense of your church, Jamaal." I ignored the second part of that statement.

I was born into this church. It was not my job to create rules of worship in this church. I had to respect and follow my elder's guidance. We were told going to school was a waste of time and resources, so I didn't go past grade seven. After all, any higher would have been too tricky to reach. I couldn't have known the importance of medicines, hospitals, doctors etc... I had to help at home, too. Girls should be married before even grade seven, and to an old church elder, especially prophets so I was lucky to get Dora. The prophets also told us going to the hospital was against God's teachings. I had also accepted that. After all, we were not

119

allowed to read the bible, so we wouldn't know what God says about it all. It's only the prophets who would tell us what God wants us to do in the church. But, I couldn't make all that a case against Death. I could only ask Life a pointed question this time.

"Do you mean the Death's thoughts that transferred into you, Life?" I queried him.

"No, Death himself." He refuses to bow down to my accusations.

"She is the one who died, not death himself. She died, Life. Dora died!"

"People always die! Especially in your church, Jamaal; you must now be used to that yourself."

"They all died, Life!"

"So, what?"

"Why did you let Death take them away?"

"Let, I didn't let anything, ask Death. I don't let anything."

"What? You mean I should ask Death why he took them away."

"Yes, since you are so good at finding who to blame, why not?" I couldn't accept that I had to blame myself, so I had to blame Death, as Life had encouraged me to do.

Dora really had to give birth unaided for the other woman in our church were always doing that. Only by prayers, that's what I had been taught, so I left her with the Midwives of our church to give birth. It was the eleventh month of her pregnancy when the baby girl now wanted to get out. Unfortunately she was so small down there. Dora couldn't force the girl out through the natural way. She groaned and whined with pain for three days without

120

pushing the elephant girl baby out. I prayed and prayed. I begged and begged God to let my wife give birth, to release her from the pain, to have the opportunity to be a father to my daughter, but on the fourth day she couldn't see that day out. The baby girl came out as bits and pieces, as bones, as smelly decaying pieces, as clotted blood throughout that afternoon. Dora died in the evenings. They let me know about that the night of that fourth day; that Death had taken them away from me.

So, what Life is saying, is that I have to ask Death why he did that to me.

Death

"Death, I haven't forgotten the smile I would love to see again; lightening and electrifying." I started tamely, not to put him off my case. I have to weave into it nicely, I told myself, after failing to get headway with Life. I had to change from the confrontational attitude that I took with Life.

"No, you haven't forgotten, the arms, hey..." So exuding with sarcasm was Death, and I couldn't help boiling, just a bit. "The arms, what arms?"

"Her arms, of-course Dora's arms, Jamaal?"

"You must know I want to be enclosed in Dora's arms and her hands all over my body, Death"

"... assuring, calming, soothing touches, hey?" I could have beaten this nonsense down Death's spine. He was such an insufferable pig, but I didn't want to be in his brood, yet. I needed answers first, so I tried to be reasonable, even though I bristled a bit, in my reply.

121

"You are making fun at me!"

"No, I am not. I am only acknowledging your truth."

Your truth! As if there were many truths. I am the one who lost them, not many other people, or truths…, so my truths must be the truth to talk about here. After losing her I left this church and haven't been to any church. I discovered they were a lot other truths in this church that I now found so naïve and stupid. This apostolic sect has, and it still has them, strange beliefs. They believed in polygamy. My younger brothers and cousins now have at least 4 wives each, and I am still alone. After Dora, I can't think of anyone else. It's crazy, maybe both ways. Like matrixes of the blind who always seek eternal forms; they also believe that even those problems that were not solved after praying, in their minds they are considered solved, like when someone dies, it was just-meant-to-be-solution, or thinking. And, it was a belief that was as rich as sin itself.

This church would have its annual Passover at Macheke, in the Mashonaland East Province. We would go there, big families to spend a month out there meditating, or not really doing that. It was also an opportunity for the old prophetic men to parade their new acquisitions, new wives, and to drink lots of tea and battered bread, singing.

"*Chingwa china majarini kuna baba.*" (*Buttered bread for the father.*)

And the men will join in.

"*Tinoda tii hobvu.*" (*We want heavily milked tea.*)

Altogether they will chorus.

"*Wanzai chingwa kuna baba.*" (*Give lots of bread to father.*)

"*Nokuti ndivo vanotenga.*" (*Because he is the one who buys.*)

"*Vane ndebvu dzakachena.*" (*He who has white beards.*)

122

"Kunenge mupunga wakaoma"   *(Like dried rice grains.)*

And their musical instruments will be their mouths, and they will create a sound into the wind like... *"Tururu, tururu, tururu, tururu, Tururu, tururu, tururu, tururu..."* Trick voices to the wind, to wind up the minds of initiate members of this church!

After singing for some time, the sun hazy hot, a sun blast on our bald heads, and tail-like beads. And, I still have old boy's beards, with worry of the past two months; it has become a little scruffy and unkempt. My towel-like-garment is slicking wet with sweat, bunched around my loins like a little kid in pampers, the legs sticking out from these pampered garments like matchsticks. I am so thirst from the heat of mid-October. I am disturbed, in this October midmorning; the midwives have told me that Dora has entered into labour.

They told me not to worry, but her pregnancy for the last two months has been a worrisome thing to me, so I can't sing well and enjoy the songs this day. But, I have no business to excuse myself to attend to my wife in labour. It is the job of midwives, so I stay with other men. Whilst singing the songs we are jibing the air up and down with our *Tsvimbos* (rods), slippery from the sweating. After singing, heartfelt, in the afternoons we recline in our shrubby shelters and drink so more tea. In this day, whilst I wait for news on Dora, other men were making love to their new wives, creating more babies, it is another of their crazy beliefs. They have to make lots and lots of babies from their lots and lots of wives. Their God told them to do so; they are helping the world, populating it. They are certainly making Pioneer seed, a growing concern.

123

I am left with worry to deal with, in our shrubby shelter. I know Dora is battling for her life now. She should have given birth by now, but nothing is forthcoming. Nobody is telling me what is happening. I have to wait. It is God's commandment! These are the truths that I had to deal with in my time of suffering, so what other truth did Death mean now?

"Just that, my truth, hey?" I asked him, I was still trying to be reasonable with Death.

"Yes, and I haven't forgotten her lovely face, the shapely form; sweet and shy as you circled them. All this was your truth again, Jamaal."

It became too obvious I wasn't getting headway with Death. Maybe, I had to face him head-on, and ask him the actual question I meant all along to ask him.

"So, why did you take them away?"

"Your Eve, I didn't take your Eve, man."

"Yes, you did." I pushed it.

"And you were Adam to her." He transgressed, intentionally trying to push me, off the case, I suppose.

"Yes, you took them away." I stilled.

"I didn't create that Eden. I am not to blame for your beliefs."

"Who did that, then?"

"You should know!"

"You, Death, must have known how much I loved those two people?"

"Of course, I know."

"You know that; even though I never came to know much about the other one, because of what you did."

124

"It's not because of me, and yes, I know."

"I used to see my unborn daughter whenever I looked at Dora, Death. She was a beautiful girl like her mother, Dora."

"What if 'she' was a boy, Jamaal?"

I couldn't answer Death that; that I knew instantly that she was a girl. I was looking forward to pouring all my loving affections on that daughter of mine. Dora and I both loved our daughter even though we never carried her in our arms.

"Killing them was as natural to you, Death; as if slaughtering fattened cows. You accomplished that in the most heartless swoop, or was that the most economical way, Death? All in one swift move- all in one gulp- all that I had loved; all that during childbirth, Death!"

"I didn't do that, I told you so already" Death bristles.

"And, I asked you who did that to me?"

"Jamaal, I think you should know!"

"I am not listening to that stupidity, how could he do that to me?"

"He did, and it's not my problem that you always have hope, man."

"Hope, hope for what?"

"For the best, from him."

"You mean its Hope that did that to me."

"I am saying it's more than that, and you should know that, Jamaal."

I should know that, *what?* That I had to spend four days hoping that she was going to be fine, that she was going to give birth to our girl. That, I was devastated on the fourth day to hear she died, that they died. No gentle transition, just an end of

125

occupation. Is this the hope Death was talking of. Maybe I should ask Hope herself.

Hope

"Why did you let me have hope, why?"

It was easier to start with Hope, than with what Death was really suggesting. Everyone always wants to have a lame duck.

"Why did you let me look forward to a wife and a child, only for you to dash that hope at the last moment?" I countered her silence with this emphasis on what she did, invoking her to reply to me, lamely.

"I don't know what you are trying to say?" She has a sweetened voice, confused; it trills sweetly into my ears, full of sweet thefts in its sweetness.

"Hope, you swallowed them in one gulp, all that I had hoped for."

"No, I didn't. You must know I am too soft to do something like that to someone. I suppose you are at the wrong door." "Were you satisfied, were you satisfied, Hope?"

"No, I didn't." She repeated her denials like the stupid thing that I have realised she was. She was just one of those untouchables, nebulous things created, recreated, and re-recreated to soften things.

"If not, why didn't you swallow me, too?"

"I didn't, please!" I liked the whine in her pathetic statement. It makes me feel a bit powerful. It's always easier to deal with Hope than with real things like Death and Life. It gives me a bit more courage to be rude to Hope.

126

"Why don't you just shut your bloody mouth and stop lying about having hope."

"I didn't say that." She was so contrite.

"You are denying such an obvious truth?" She just shrugs her shoulders, obviously defeated, and deflated; losing her bloody hope in me.

"Please don't just shrug your shoulders as if you haven't heard me. Why didn't you say 'No' when they were being lowered in your yawning but beautiful mouth, Hope?"

"No, but 'No' to what, Jamaal?" She has found her voice, once again, but it is a small voice, a girl's voice, Dora's voice.

"You didn't!"

"Do what? I didn't swallow them, it's the..." I liked the captured voice I could feel in her protests, but didn't like the path she was beginning to tread on with her statement, so I cut her off.

"No, please stop that! Don't even think of saying it; that it was the grave that swallowed them."

"You are the one who buried them into the grave, Jamaal." I am surprised by such strength, but I could only question her...

"Me! No! You are the one who did that, and you only did that hope thing of yours when they were safely inside you, and when you knew they would never leave you."

"What hope thing?"

"Stop mouthing the obvious."

"What hope thing?" She is closer to tears.

"That thing you are doing right now." I am closer to tears too. I have to find strength, to staunch off the tears.

127

"What am I doing?" She is now sneezing quietly to herself. It seems it's me who's sneezing.

"The hope thing!?"

"What?" I can barely hear her.

"Prove me if I am wrong, Hope. Puke them out! Just do it! Puke them out for me, Hope!" I am angry with myself, with the tears.

"Ask the grave you lowered them into to do that for you. You are stupid!" Such strength is coming after the tears, so amazing!

"You wouldn't dare, Hope!" I had to leave her be. I wasn't getting any headway with Hope. I didn't like tears anymore; I didn't like seeing that kind of water flowing down my cheeks, again. I had cried enough. I didn't have a lot of time to waste on excuses of things like Hope. I had to time things with Time, himself: Time; as an internal presence, in which experience is embedded in the material vestiges of our lives.

Time

"You Time, you started assuring me and telling me that it was not your fault, neither the fault of Death, Hope, and Life."

This didn't seem enough to go with Time. He started treading that well worn path I didn't want him to tread, yet. He said to me."It was God's fault." There, the bolt was out on the open. Then, he refracted from it, he said, talking as of something else, but using his time script.

"Their time here was up." And, I couldn't help boil.

"Shame on you...! Shame on you, Time!"

128

Why would he do a thing and then, pass the buck on someone else? What time was he talking of. He is a lie, Time is! He is a big fat liar, Time is!

"It was God's fault," and then in another parallel he is saying, "Their time here was up."

He is such a liar!

God

The God I know couldn't have done such a thing, a thing that makes me so sad, because he loves me. HE started lying to me about time changing all that in a long run. Shame on you! That-: HE just couldn't help blazing into a rage like a hummingbird, slamming into a clean and well washed window? How could Time, Hope, Death, and Life have helped me when they were in this with HIM from the beginning? It is three years now, and what have they done to the pain, God?

Pain

Pain, and his godhood clustering of sorrow and depressive moods are still there, so poignantly and so profoundly felt. Pain is still crimson bright in me, wrecking havoc every day, killing me slowly, pushing me towards damnation. Tears flow unimpeded whenever I am alone. Dora left a deep yawning void in my heart. All these tears that I have shed don't seem to be filling it up. Instead, it seems like every drop of tear that I have shed has fallen into this void, not filling it up. They say it will change,

129

when and how about now? How about the suffering and the eating away now?

Memories

When I think of them, the memories brings so much pain and sorrow in my heart. I get hurt again and again.

"It will improve. The memories will be better, some day."

Someone among that bunch of liars says that to me. (S)he doesn't even realise that this bruise inside me is now like a stem of an unknown flower, smelling of acid burning in my heart and soul. I now survive by resisting the abrasive bitter-taste of the thoughts of her, which are like an amour-plated catfish swimming through my head, leaving behind painful scales and barbells, like decaying teeth that aches and gets all the worse as long as nothing is done to remove them. Every night, I think of them, I would lie wide awake into the small hours of morning.

*****   *****

All this is nothing to the uncaring you Life, Memories, Death, Life, Hope, and to you, God.

"But we understand." They chorus, inanely.

"If you did care for me you couldn't have done what you did, Death, had you cared, just a little bit..."

"I didn't do anything!" Death, the sole ruler-supreme, he didn't do anything?!

"Just a little bit of time is what I needed, Time."

130

"You have all the time in the world to find your path again." He times his replies. He is talking of having dreams, a new life, and new direction. Dreams- things like interpretations, false trails- the ill-fitting labels of standard definitions, making dreams. He must know it's the mind alone that's equipped to create dreams, to do dreaming...

"Bring her back, God?"

"What has happened has happened. I took what belonged to me. You belong to me, too." Such omnipresence, omniscience, omnipotence primal awareness!

"Bring them back to me if you care a little bit about my memories."

"If I bring them back to you, you won't have those memories."

"It's Ok to lose them, I want her hope!" It was better to turn into an informal life, or informal surviving, or even informal existence..., a life without memories, just to have her back with me.

"You have her hopes." Hope tries to sweeten the pill, as usual.

"I need her love!"

"You will find others to love." Memories cusses.

"I love her, you, Life!"

"You will love others." Life copies Memories' adage.

"Oh, how I miss her, oh my God!"

"Man always misses what he can't have anymore!" And, that's GOD

131

I really do miss her so very, very much! And, I only hope that the bunch of you would give outmost attention to my request.

Sincerely, yours

Jamaal A. Mukonomushava

NB:
There shouldn't be that polemical debate among you to engage in, on how to calculate the value of life, or a nebulous take-on at forgetting or precisely its sainted better-half-: forgiveness, but just a deeply felt demand for you to bring her back to me.

THE LIVING ROOM

The living room that is not
The room to loom, to leave
Reserved for the living
When to live is not a sacrifice

A sacrificial pedestal for the unliving:
Abstract paintings, unused chessboard, expensive picture frames,
a lot without photos in them, one with a very old photo, one with
her photo, one with an unknown girl, framed inside it…it's a
picture frame. The unknown girl is praying, in a prayer, like as if
before prayer. Lilith? Garden Eden isn't that. Plastic plants, liquor
cabinets; with unopened bottles, maturing beer… And wine. A
calendar from long ago, counting life backwards, or is it time,
backwards? What time is it? 1 am, it's I: AM in the morning.
Nearby a pot of sand, in it, a frozen wax candle, as if a bird was
trying to pick out its own heart, with its own death beak: death,
dead, die. Did she? He thinks, in the dead form, *she is my mom. My
mom who is still alive.*
Death, dead, die….

Death's waters
In her religion they cooked food using water sipped after cleaning
her body. They couldn't stay (the mourning woman of the street)
for the food, to eat her. And, her family was supplying endless
foods but there was no one left to eat her. It was witch's food. It
had been cooked using the witch's waters. The place became an
unwanted or unappreciated restaurant in a ghost city.

133

The living room is still
Its contents do not move
Make sounds, they do not!

A door, to door it
There is only one door: a back door into it or out of it; into the
living room, out of the living room. Doors! To door in. There is
no front door. To front in. Had there ever been a front door?
Front. He sees where it should have been. Where it should have
been, there is a glass door. He walks to it. It is the light from the
mirror, which collects him in, into the landscape of this room. He
presses his face against the glass of it, all that unrealised potential.
He tries to open the glass door, but it is locked. He thought of
breaking it, with his body, for broken glass predicts change,
necessarily not beneficial, but he thought better of it. So, he
doesn't break it. He will keep the glass mirror, for glass generally
indicates a strong psychic or intuitive ability. He tries to open the
glass door, but it is locked.

He goes back to get the keys.
The act of going back goes with him
It never returns back with him.
He goes back to unlock it, but it is already unlocked.
He is unlocked, he must be doors or
There must be another lock on the outside, he thinks.

The unused chessboard

134

He retires back into the room. He sits on the wasted grey sofa. It has stripes of greys and smaller stripes of greens that interlocks. Flowery grey. He sleeps on a couch right across the sofa he is sitting on, smaller for his long frame, so nights he sleeps on bended knees. His blankets and clothing rests on this couch, like left over dreams. He takes the chessboard, opens it. Note: the lack of him in *open it*. He populates it with ponies on the back lines, and the others (horses, bishops, castles, a queen, a king, these; always competing in the hashed silence like cotton, by sheer will they always put themselves at the back row).
Today he puts them on the front. He wills it!

We pray to space by doing life
On the opposing side, he leaves that space open. Space is Open. Open space is a double negative, it's a positive possibility. Space denotes the world before mathematical exactitude, and the world of mathematical doubt. We play with (pray to) space by doing life. He is playing chess against himself. He jumps the pony, taught (thought) better of it, and he returns it back. He remembers; it's the horse that should jump around. Horses...
So he lets one of his horses jump...it's a long, long leap. To leap is an act of freedom. It lands well beyond her characters..., playing her things out of the game.

He waits. What colour is waiting??
When the silence starts dominating, he looks at the mirror door, the glass doors where a door should have been, was, is...

Do tears make moaning sounds?
135

The face on the window, dissolving, reconstituting, he doesn't like the look of the thing that looks back at him. The look of the door that looks back at him overwhelms his ability to tell her to play her move. Cold, eternal, eyes of black marble: tears trying, beginning to appear. Do tears make moaning sounds? Whoaaa, whoaaa, whoaaa… howling out a glossolalia over her death?

This living room was empty (that was empty) with a swarm of relatives, a month ago. His father, with tears in his heart, said, *The light thing has taken her.* He meant, he now thinks but doesn't know for sure, what he meant was, *nothing is more orderly than nothing.* Maybe he meant, *The dark thing has taken her.*
Is nothing more orderly than nothing?
We are always tied down to eye-blink half-lives. Blink blink, unsure of who or how to hold hard.

There is nothing to hold, there is no outside world, only a mirror…and the outside that is not a world. He is inside excavated-out time; phantom wind excites the outside, which is not there, perhaps; it's a slow shadow, passing. And an unseen silhouette on his mind obstructs him.

He reverts his eyes, back onto the chessboard.
She has played her hand…no, no, no…it's a move…he tells himself. Lazy eight!

This is not crazy eight!
He sits back on the vehicle of his imaginations, seeing her skip a couple of gears with her castle, accelerate with the bishop, lose

136

grip with the pony, crash with another pony, as it lands square feet beside his queen: checkmate! The little men of the war have done their work, sacrificed for the good of the big man. She says *Checkmate,* again, she is smiling, smirking at him, her smile stinking him like a newborn's first wound, or the shock of birth. No wound prepares human beings for the loneliness in the world they empty into at birth than that first wound of birth: Birth itself! Herself. He stares at her smile again, it's a life. She is life. It is life.

It belongs to the outside, rubbing out the blooded outside air… She sets out to stop the air outside from hemorrhaging berries, or blood…

With her smile, of course!

Not with words
When she was here with him she would talk and talk, and it's now amazing that with so many words in her being, she hasn't set one free. Why not make use of her key (words) to utter nothing: to soften this myth machine in him, anger, the bull brute cry, bonfire as this azure, or maybe a spatula; a wedge to be woven in…

Now she is saying to ask questions and she will participate, and he says to her:

I can't get through the glass!

He cannot leave this room, live in this house…loom, room out of this room. He has taken time further inland; to sew lives' boats, thoughts' ships, and feelings' vessels. Everything floats: rugs, tables, chairs- and so do his dreams, dry fields of corn, dry

137

riverbeds in the draught year of 1992. Everything: browner, greying, decaying…
1992, that's when he met her,

2002- Everything: browner, greying…
He no longer leaves the living room: only for smashing the singles, not for bathing, not for the albums. He doesn't bath anymore, for a month no water knows the surface of his outer crusts. There is a toilet, off this living room for the singles charts. He packed his shelves with edibles, non-perishables, ready to eat non-nourishables.
He barely eats.
He is shallow, sallow; like the skinny, yellow sheaves of wheat sprouting inside the sun deprived damp granaries, lacking in character, self-interested, contractive, unintelligible….
He is trapped
He leaves the chessboard alone, unused, on the wasted grey sofa.

He fishes his old Mbira instrument among his stuff on the couch, a warped Nyunganyunga thing. *Mbira music?* Now it has only three out of seven, of its keys left on the upper row. And two middle keys on the lower row. He touches the upper keys with his fingertips, puffs of dust music rose off its gourd inlaid belly, dusty sounds- a strange primitive melody rivers out of the keys, and then he deepens it with the lower two deep keys. He feels, with each touch of the keys, as if he is drawing circles on top of the river's waters.

The forked shadow of music, an echo, a decaying interval, a beginning, a blue shift delayed, as he jumps those empty places were other keys should have.

Her space, in his life, is like those empty places where other keys are supposed to be, creating silent silences, silent musics.

And when the last note dies, silence rules.

The silence's music finds him shoring up against a loss, a loss that isn't there!

Talking silences? Talking music!

Talking silences, musical silences?

He is dying

He is dying himself, and inside him, he feels that quick, sour blackness, but the greying edges are worn out so finely, that he has got a sinkhole in him that whistles clean.

There is only yesterday and now- tomorrow sneezes in a broken triangular shape whose name he would kill to learn.

There is no outside, only inside

. . . .

Rooms

Looms

Walls

Holes

Mirror

Mirror

. . . .

ECLIPSE

"Oh no, no, no, no! Oh no! Momma, no, no, no please Uncle! You are hurting me Uncle. *Oh! Yowee! Maiwe kani!* Oh my! Oh my! Uncle what are you doing? Please let me from under you. Please, please. Your weight is too much for me. Please, I am begging you please, please...!" I am crying all I can, shrieking all I can, and entreating him to let me go, but all that is in vain. I know nobody would hear us, for the next household is some hundreds of metres away. Not to mention, we are in the kitchen with a closed door so whatever noise I am making isn't going too far.

In the past few months of our stay together, I thought my Uncle liked me a lot because he always had his eyes on me. I felt so liked and so loved. However, I began to suspect that there was something wrong with his overwhelming attention towards me as I realized that he never looked me in the eyes, but at my buttocks, my small stone breasts, and private parts. The looks he gave me were also not friendly, but rather insolent, malicious, and dreamy, as if he was in a private conversation with my body. What got me distrustful of those looks was because he only gave me those looks whenever we were alone or when no one else was paying attention.

Later, his hands were on my body as if he didn't know they were there. He would playfully touch my breast. When I give him a disturbed questioning look, he would smile in a deceitful way as if I liked what he was doing. Whenever I bring him something, he wouldn't take the thing without touching me. I was afraid of

140

telling Momma; she couldn't really have understood. She would have thought I was only trying to make trouble for her brother. I had once told Mother that I didn't like her brother. But, I hadn't told her why I didn't like him. She would have thought I just didn't like him because of anything that he had done, but just because I was jealous of him.

I started to avoid him successfully. When I knew in advance that Mother would be away, I found someplace else to go. I only returned when I was so sure Momma was back. I played this cat and mouse game for nearly a month. After a while, I began to think he had changed his mind and would leave me alone. When I came home from school, I found him alone. He told me that Mother had gone to the local shopping centre for important meetings. He took a day-off from his work to baby-sit me and the house while Mother was gone. At first, I wanted to run as fast as I could away from home. As if he read my mind, he told me that he was going out fishing. He took the fishing gears and some bait and went to Nyajezi River. About half an hour later, he came back with an excuse that the water was too muddy to fish. But, the funny thing was, though, that it hadn't rained in over a week. *How could the river still be muddy?*

He came into the kitchen where I was busy sweeping the floors and closed the door. I felt like screaming, but he told me that he didn't mean any harm and, that it was too windy to sweep the dirt out. I continued sweeping while darting some fearful glances at him. He just quietly sat on the cement and brick bench that surrounded the better half of the kitchen, staring into the roof. When I came to sweep where he was sited, he grabbed my hands and told me that he had a game in mind, and wanted to play with me.

At first, I thought he really meant it. It didn't take long for his hands to start straying all over my body. When I told him that I would scream if he doesn't stop touching me or tell Momma when she comes back. He suddenly stopped what he was doing and started to strangle my throat. With his hands painfully squeezing my throat, he told me that if I ever were to tell anyone, then he would kill me with his knife. He took a knife out of his trousers' side pockets and told me to remain silent if I wanted to live.

Out of terror and desperation, I remained silent as he grabbed my tender breasts. Then, he touched my buttocks and intimate part. I felt his hands searching around my internal moistness as if he was hunting for a secret. He was groaning badly. He pushed me down to the floors... Uncle had lost his power of speech, his power of hearing anything but could only rant and gnash his teeth and pin me down under his huge body. In a moment of fury he tore my clothes despite these entreaties from me and then my undergarments.

I knew he was going to violate me. In desperation, I started to really struggle and fight him. Like a tick to a cow my Uncle stuck on me. With furious raw power, he got hold of my hands and tucked them in his own hands which were so strong. He was beyond understanding, beyond control, beyond the touch of anything else other than this task at hand. I was under him and nothing else mattered to him; nothing else should have come into reckoning with him. It didn't really matter to him that I was also

142

human. He entered me, however young, with all the raw force in his loins.

He ravaged my womanly, destroying it and damaging it to a messy of blood and pulpy tissues. After he had satisfied his murderous intention, and ejaculated all his manly into me, he urinated into my painful, sour, bleeding womanly. Finally, he moved out of me with so much satisfaction showing on his face. To him, I didn't have a heart, a mind, or soul; therefore, I didn't deserve respect and dignity. When he saw me still crying, he beat his tracks out of our home without a word or a check at the hurt that he had inflicted upon me. He ran away before the hand of the law struck him.

What was my mother thinking inviting this disgusting man into our house? Why had my Uncle raped me? What did I do to deserve such pain?

I was still crying when Momma returned from Nyatate. Although I was still crying, it was dry tears I was crying for a hallow ache had seeped into my chest. When Momma found me on the floor bleeding from my intimate part, she asked me who had done that to me. I told her it was her brother. Mother, being afraid of the consequences that would befall all of her brother's family, told me to not discuss this with anyone, not even with my own family members. If this story were to get out, then he would be jailed for up to seven years. His family would lose a breadwinner.

After the incident, I was afraid of socialising with people, even with kids of my age. I didn't want to go outside the house at all. My brother and sister tried to encourage me to go out and have fun with them, but I wasn't interested in the games anymore. I knew I couldn't go back to the old days anymore. I

143

just wanted to be left alone. Momma tried to encourage me to go out too, but didn't succeed. She didn't pressure me, though. I knew that Momma cared about what had befallen me. I saw her crying when she was alone. I knew she was hurt, but I also reeled from my own suffering. I couldn't go to the hospital in order to keep the secret. There was so much damage on my private part. Sometimes, I bled profusely if I did anything compromising to my still tender, soar, and painful part. I wondered whether I could ever heal. I kind of knew I will never have a man in my life or have kids of my own!

One night, I woke up in the middle of the night and saw my mother crying silently by my bed side. I realized that Momma was there because I cried for help in my dream. After the day I was raped, I've been having nightmares every night. In my dream, I hear him coming for me. He tells me not to worry, and that he doesn't mean any harm. I can't sit there and wait to be caught by him. So, I start running. He chases me and tells me to wait for him in his chilling voice. Then, he laughs loudly in his howling crackling voice but his voice feels like the wailing-thin sound of the mad siren enclosed in a vast bottomless pit. I am the only one who feels the pain in the voice because all its sharp laughter's stabs are points at me. He says, in his laughter, in his voice, that it is hopeless for me to run away because he will surely catch me and defile me again and again. I can barely breathe when I think of what he will do to me again if he catches me. At the end, he catches me.

He is gloating and ranting like a wild boar as he wrecks my tender womanly with his big male as if he has turned crazy. The more I am crying, the more he is pounding onto me. He seems

144

to be thinking that I am enjoying it. This whips his lusting into an all-out war. I stop crying, but that doesn't seem to stop him either. He smashes and smashes into me; he enters and enters into me, deeper and deeper, tearing me, jibing me, wrecking me through and through. He seems to want to murder me by strangling, but he seems not to find the object to rend this cold rage inside his bosom against. But, he has the object to direct the full wrath of his murderous intentions.

I am almost suffering from suffocation, from the pain. I cry out for help. This is when I would call for Momma to protect me from being raped again. On nights such as this, my cries are the little grasps of the butterflies.

Every night, no matter how hard I try to unconsciously rein these dreams away, the visions still float to me. These images disturb me. I would breathe in and out and shut my eyes out until I scrub the dreams out of my mind, but they would return back when I go to sleep again. Momma has been staying in my bedroom, almost every night in order to assure me that there was no one chasing me. My brother and sister were also spending sleepless nights puzzled about what had become of me. There was nothing I could do about that. I knew they were hurt because they loved me. Part of me felt guilty for their pain. I seethed over the guilt and shame I was suffering from. I think it was particularly hurtful to Momma to watch all of us suffering. She was also afraid to report the horrible incident to the police because she believed that it could destroy my life, if the public became conversed with the details of the rape case.

I didn't want to worry about all that; I craved for distraction, just for a couple of minutes, to be unaware of it all. I agreed with

145

Momma; I wanted to rest, I wanted quietness, and most of all, I wanted to be myself again. I wanted everyone to leave me alone, especially my Uncle in the terrifying dreams. Momma severed any communications with her brother. She directly told him in a letter that she didn't want to see him for as long as she lived. I now shied away from male-company, especially if they have high howling voices like my Uncle's. I didn't want to be left alone with a man in a private place. I also refused to accompany young girls of my age out for fun. They were so happy and full of life. I couldn't be happy like them, no matter how hard I tried.

Telling anyone how I felt was beyond my imagination. How could I have told anyone about those horrible memories? How could I have told them that being near by a man reminds me of those vivid memories of my Uncle? Any form of physical touch by a man, no matter how innocent it was, always took me back to the day of which my Uncle repulsively caressed me and entered my private part. How could I have told anyone, even Momma, about the pain and anger? Tell me, how could I? No one could have known how I felt. Words can't describe my pain. It towers beyond imaginations and understanding. Talking about it could have changed my life. I just didn't want to welcome more tears or pain. It is too much for me to handle.

So, I had to shut myself out tight so that I won't be probed again. I even thought of this hallow ache in my heart as a closed box, enclosing my heart in it. I have to keep these hurts and emotions under ice, under this darkness, in this box. In this way, I could, at least, live and be as much of me as possible despite the eternal darkness that now envelops the horizons of my once colourful

146

life. Despite the fact that this hallow ache that encloses my heart feels so suspiciously empty and dark like a hospital room when the shades are drawn, the windows darkened, light sensitive, death burdened. What jail term could have paid for all that? Seven years of jail sentence! Could it have helped me escape from an eternal life in the darkness? Could the sun have shined its rays once more? Could it have made the painful memories go away? Could it have helped me forgive Momma for telling me not to report him to the police? Only if it frees me from the darkness and let me be myself again...

But, when would I stop surviving my days and start living them?

LIKE THE SUN RISING.

I knocked on the door again.

"Yes, I am coming."

That's his voice. So, he is home. How am I going to start apologising to him about yesterday? He opens the door and he is surprised to see me there.

"Catherine!"

"Hello Joel.., may I come in, please?"

"Yes, of course you can come in."

He opens the door wider and steps aside to let me in. "Come in please."

I take the armchair near the window and wait for him to settle on the other one near the door. Unexpectedly, he comes and sits on the bed, which should have been too closer for my own liking yesterday. But, it doesn't bother me today. He says.

"About yesterday...?"

"No, don't blame yourself. I should be the one to blame, Joel."

"I was too forward." He offers.

"No, you were not, Joe."

I'm surprised with myself for saying this without blushing. In other circumstances, I couldn't have had courage to say something like this. He looks surprised too. As if he is trying not to comment on my behaviour, he offers refreshments.

"What can I offer you Cathy? Tea, coffee, or drinks?"

"Coffee please, black."

148

"Sugar?"

"Nope."

He comes back with two cups of coffee. After handing me one, he takes his to the bed. We are sipping the coffee, silently engrossed in our thoughts. I feel I really have to make an effort. I promised myself last night that I would make an effort. I spent that entire night thinking about what had transpired the yesterday afternoon. How many times have I resisted affections? How many times have I been afraid of being probed and abandoned in a dark place again? Despite all those painful memories, I still felt it was about time I should really start loving someone. I knew I have to let go those hurtful memories soon or later which had always beclouded me from being intimate with someone. This time, I want to put my best effort and have a nice relationship with Joel.

Those sick and painful memories had come between us when Joel tried to kiss me yesterday. Instantly, I felt sick to my stomach, feeling extremely nauseous. I fled to the bathroom covering the mouth with my hand. In the toilet, I had to let it go. I didn't have to fight it. Because the force was so strong, I puked up through my mouth and nose.

Joel came to the bathroom and tried to comfort me by holding me. I felt like I was in that dark room again. I elbowed him away and ran out of the bathroom. Last night, I had come to a conclusion that the best way to deal with my fear was to face those horrible feelings. I still feel embarrassed about what happened in the bathroom yesterday. I rejected Joel while he was trying to help me. I let this happen to myself.

Joel is very sensitive and delicate; he deserves the best from me. I also know he loves me deeply. I feel the same way about him too. I have to open myself up so that Joel can enter into my heart. I must let go of the sick feeling inside me which stops me from being physically affectionate with someone. Joe's really special. I don't want to mess this one up. I am finally tired of fighting back my feelings for him. I realised that there was no sense of fear in me, but only determination.

"Joel, I think there is something very important you should know about me."

"What about you, Cathy?"

"Something that happened to me during my secondary school years."

"Yes, what is it, Cathy?"

"We were in the last term of our "O" levels, at Mapako secondary school. Our teacher, Mr Chinembiri, asked me to bring the books to the staff room one day. I had to wait for the last student to finish his work to get the books. It was dark by the time I brought the books to his house because the Stuff room had then been locked. When I knocked on his door, he told me to bring the books inside. If I had known what was going to happen to me that evening, then I would never have entered his house. Since he was my teacher, I really didn't think that he had any other intentions."

"Intentions! Do you mean..." Joel murmurs and searches my eyes.

"Yes..., he raped me, Joe."

That's all that I could manage to say to him. I still felt I had to protect everyone from the grisly details.

"Oh my goodness, I am so sorry, Cathy." He comes close to where I was and takes my hands. He holds my hands with care.

"What happened to the teacher? Did you report him?"

"Yes."

I told him that the teacher was sentenced to seven years in prison. He was also banned from teaching anywhere in the country.

"That's not enough. He should have been given a much more severe punishment."

He seems visibly angry. I have never seen him upset like this before. *He really must care a whole-lot about me?* "If I find this man, then I am going to tear him into pieces with my bare hands. He deserves it. He shouldn't have taken advantage of your trust. He was your teacher. He should have cared for his students like a parent. I can't imagine what the whole education system would become of? It just bugs the hell out of me!"

After a moment of silence, he probed me, sensitively. "So, when I touched you yesterday, it sort of invoked all those bad memories?"

"Yes. But, that doesn't mean that I want you to stop showing me your affection. You know I love you Joe. I want to get rid of those horrible memories. I need you in my life, Joe. I hope that you don't feel differently about me because of what happened yesterday. Please forgive me if I hurt you."

"No, you don't have to apologise for it, Cathy. I now understand everything."

"So?" I inquired.

"So what? Oh! You think that I changed my mind about you, do you?" I nod in agreement to his observation.

"Not in a million years, babe; not in this lifetime; or not in another lifetime, I love you so much. I am here for you. Nothing can change the way I feel about you. Nothing! Do you hear me, Cathy? Nothing!"

He held me in his arms and said, "I am going to give you all of my love. All of it, Cathy! More than I have ever thought I can possibly give to someone."

I bore deeper into his arms for protection. I knew that he would never hurt me. I knew I couldn't let him go. I knew the woman he loved was still in me. I knew I would eventually be able to trust someone. There is hope for a new life without fear and hatred in me.

AIN'T THE ONE

Charlotte had the courage after a while and asked him.

"How many girls have you dated before me, David?"

And he answered her flippantly as if he hadn't care about not even a single one of those girls.

"I stopped counting at 13."

"Oh!" That's what Charlotte could only say.

He knew what that "oh!" meant. It meant that he had slept with each and every one of those thirteen girls. In her eyes, he was a male-whore. David didn't care enough to explain to her that it hadn't really been all of that.

"So, why didn't you marry one of those thirteen girls, Dave?" It's a question that she kept repeating over and over. Each and every of those times, he wondered what she really was trying to mine from him with such a question.

"I wasn't ready to settle down."

Or: "I was waiting for the right girl, and now that you are here, I can marry."

Maybe: "I needed time to mature more."

These answers would bring the jibe that he could never really be mature. All those answers never satisfied her for she didn't stop mining him for more answers to that question.

The other time, Charlotte jokingly said that he could never marry, ever. Later, it became her national anthem, and that he

153

had some evil spirit within him that fought with him whenever he thought of marrying. Also, she thought he was considering her as an appeasement to this evil spirit. By dating her, she thought that he could satiate this purported spirit of hers. One other time, he really wanted to laugh at her face until he was crazy for thinking like that, but most of the times, it just made him irritated and sometimes angry with her. He couldn't shout at her when he stopped counting was when he was in his middle twenties and that over the years that he had severally been in love and out of love.

Maybe, what pinched her was the fact that since he had stopped counting she was never to be on the number-line of his loves. It would be like she had never really happened in his life because he couldn't count her to the next girl as well, as if there was never to be another girl after her! As if her words had nothing to do with her!

In the soft underside of David's emotions, he has always been a sucker for pleasing Charlotte. So, he lied to her that they hadn't been that many girls over the years, and that most of those girls he hadn't felt much for, if he felt anything for them, and that it was her that he loved. But over the years, his boy's hopes and dreams had gone blue. His heart was now a broken treaty.

All the girls that he had dated in his late teens and early twenties only thought about marriage. They thought that if he said he loved them, or if he were dating them, then automatically, he would have to marry them. They worked him around getting to talk and decide about marriage. It also meant that they were never to put any more effort in the relationship because marriage was

154

already a given. David has always scarred away from these girls the moment he figures out that about them. They were also those who thought he wasn't good enough for them.

"Where would I hide that big fat nose of yours, David?" One of those girls asked him. He felt so bad, so ugly. He would really like to have said to her:

"Why, on your beautiful sweet face, babe!" But, he couldn't say that because he was hurting. When David was hurting he would freeze, so he was frozen. Her beauty; her unfulfilled love, her laughter at him, her lack of belief in him for some time lived in the space containing him. She lived in the things that he wanted. Sometimes the things that he wanted were there in her, sometimes they were not there. Other times David thought he was both the things he wanted and the things he didn't want in her. Looking into his own reflection, in the bathroom mirror, David knows he is handsome. He doesn't care what others think of him. Now, he doesn't really give a shit. He doesn't give a bloody-shit! He would have told this girl off,

"The boy you are interested in is the one standing next to me, not me. He likes the attention that you are giving him. He thinks he is a great guy just because you are beautiful and also because you have told him that he is handsome. But, I have learned the harder way that it doesn't really make you or him any better than I am or better than the next girl or boy." And he would have continued, unafraid of what this bluntness would elicit from her.

"Probably, you are beautiful and probably he is handsome, too. I am not interested for I have no intentions of being anything other than who I am." But he couldn't say all that to that girl, back then.

155

Now, he knew he had no intention of wearing polo-shirts and brown loafers, and be pompous to that girl of his who had told him that he was ugly. He had no intentions of being a male-queen, even for Charlotte. Now, he has also realised that he doesn't even need a woman, a wife, or even at that, children, to make him complete, no!

There was this gorgeous babe that he dated casually for a couple of months in one of his drifting times. They were attending the same marketing class, at Herentals College, in central Harare. She used to hang out with him because she needed help with her studies. As they studied together, they sort of drifted into a relationship. David doesn't even know how they got to that for she seemed exactly the kind of girl that he wouldn't have dated. Yet, there he was with a pink-kind-of-a-girl. He used to banter with her and called her "kasalad", which means that she was simply uncooked like salad. Salad girls only care about their looks and money. They are usually as empty as the blue skies. After getting to know a little more about her, David discovered that she was more than "kasalad."

"Can I come over to your workplace for lunch, David?" "David, will you please buy me lunch today?" "You never spent money on me, Dave." "Dave, you are so stingy. How can I love you, David?" "David, you have got to feed me if I am your babe." "David that, David this, Dave that, Dave this…" Money, money, and money!

All these pinpricks nettled him to damnation. The more she prickled for money, the more he hardened toward her. Eventually, he began really enjoying saying "no" to her, especially

156

when she asked him to spend money on her. It became like as if his mind was programmed to say "no." This relationship didn't last long. It didn't bother him that much though when she left him for another guy who was more accommodative of her material wishes. David is glad that he didn't have to continue wasting his feelings on her!

He has always been a difficult person, especially with girls he would be dating. Deep down he is all a soft puddle for love, like a puppy. Since love is such a monster, and since it was easy to misuse and be misused in love, David has always left a part of him out of love or a relationship. This part has always been his devil's advocate, looking at a girl's intentions. What she is after in regards to what he had for her. He does seem like bad sport, doesn't he? But, someone you love can burn down your home without a care. Then return with the ashes of your feelings in her hands, a small pile in her hands, of all of your love for her. And, there are a lot other ways people who are in love can hurt each other without even meaning to. David discovered that in the middle of his twenties.

There was this girl that he dated. The girl was well liked by his family and friends. As she was overly concerned with being liked by his family and friends, all she spent her energy and time more on them than him. David felt neglected by her. She acted the coy to damnation. This behaviour of hers nettled him for some time. He even shared his concern with her. She promised him that she would work toward making their relationship tighter, but never showed any change. A few months into their relationship, he was ill with cholera for over a week. Although she was told by his friends that he was ill, she never came to see

157

how he was doing. Acting all the prim and coy! David supposes, also acting the good church girl who doesn't go to the boyfriend's place without a chaperon. When David got better that's when she came to see him with other church-mates. He told her straight away that he was no longer interested in her. He had also figured out that there was very little frosting in the relationship to hold them together down the road.

She tried to convince his sisters and friends behind his back to get back with him. He had had enough of her. What he never told anyone was how badly hurt he was that she had neglected him in his time of need.

David also dated a girl who stole his first kiss. *Jaysus*, Mary, and Joseph! This girl was so wicked with her mouth. David wondered where she learned all that stuff that she was doing with her tongue. Her mouth ignited sparks and flash points throughout his body. She kissed him with so much passion that left him melting inside. He was madly in love with her. Unfortunately, at the end of her month of stay with her cousins, she left without even a goodbye. She didn't even leave her telephone number. He felt dumped and hurt for a while. He had no choice, but simply, to let her go.

We always have choices in life, but prefer to create prison cells for ourselves and put our hearts on the floors of hell trying to live our lives for the other person. By trying too harder to see how good we can love them, and how better placed we have been in the scheme of things like love. Sometimes, we psyche ourselves out and walk through the blocked streets of their

158

hearts, avoiding traffic in and out of those streets and, dealing with the micro-motions of these hearts that we pander for.

One particular girl, who was his sister's friend, went to the extent of telling his sister that David was number seven on the scheme of her heart. The funny thing was that he really pined for her, but eventually he discovered that in many instances in life we take ourselves too much for granted and fail to be true to ourselves. She taught him this, another girl that he dated but had special feelings for his best friend instead. She couched this interest in the name of friendship. So, he was dating again. It was the most awkward attempt that he had ever made, everything seemed so literal. David and his friend discussed her. His friend told him that she made a pass, but found out that he was taken. David never confronted her about it. When she left for college, he knew their relationship wasn't going any further than it was. Regardless, he wrote her a couple of times.

She replied to one of the letters that David wrote. Her letter was quite deep. It was about how she thought David and his friend were taking her for granted, that both David and his friend were dogs for wanting her at the same time. David kept that letter for years to come, not because of what it reminded him of, but because of the strength and strangeness; strange in a beautiful way. For years he read it over and over again, trying to make sense of the obvious sense that was in the letter. He believed each line that came in her handwriting in that letter. It even troubled him a little bit that she was seven years younger than he was, but was making a lot of sense than he was doing at that time.

159

Now, he understands what she really meant even though he is still not so sure it was relevant.

That was the last time that he counted how many girlfriends that he had dated. She was his thirteenth girlfriend. He couldn't count all the other girls to Charlotte because the other girls hadn't amounted to anything much and he didn't care anymore to keep track of the numbers by the time he met Charlotte. He couldn't have told Charlotte how he had loved and bled badly to make himself loved by these girls. He couldn't tell her that he discovered this the hard way that they ain't the one for him. People come into our lives. Sometimes, all they do is to waste away before our eyes. After some time, we discover that they hadn't really meant that much to us.

He didn't want Charlotte to think that he also felt that she ain't the one for him.

A REVOLVING CAGE?

Charlotte came over to Chitungwiza Friday night and spent the weekend at her brother's place in the Seke Suburb of Unit C. They had agreed they would see each other at the church on Sunday. It was a bit of a crack-thing to negotiate for this compromise with her. He met her three years before. Even to negotiate for a date with her was a crack-thing. It was a fucking job interview! The moment he met her, he discovered she had the mark of the one who would be stubborn.

After church, David had waited for her like a dog waiting for its owner to come over and pat and ruffle its sheaves of hair.

Maybe, he thought, "I should bark a little bit like a dog and take no responsibility for the noise." Just like death, she hadn't been taking responsibility for the way she had been mistreating him over the years. There was nothing he could do about it, other than waiting for her. David didn't even know what would become of that waiting. He also knew that it was even possible for her to come and say, nonchalantly.

"No, I don't want to see you", or apologetically, "No, I am busy for that", or business like, the accountant that she wanted to be, "No, I do not have any prior arrangements with you about that", or forgetfully, "No, I don't remember agreeing to that". Regardless, David waited all the same.

A thick raw of marigolds along the church's yard fence are a fierce dark orange and burnt orange and the rhubarb plant near the gates where he is standing is bright clear orange and sunshine yellow. They have turned their faces towards the yard walls for some mysterious reason. Maybe, so that David won't be able to appreciate their beauty! He listens to the sound of the bees and tunes their musical instruments according to what he is hearing. Deep down, he is watching, listening, and imitating the bees' reaction to the flowers, even as they walk away from the flowers, they continue playing their songs. He remembers his grandfather who was so good at harvesting the bees' honey saying that if you can manage to imitate the bees' music you can also be able to put a swarm of bees and the queen bee into a trance and take away its honey without killing not even a single bee. David couldn't also help thinking that there were people in life who would never really appreciate others; the love they would be getting, or even the love they have for the other person.

Somehow, they are distorted. If you give them a flower, then they would throw it in the dustbin, without even smelling it. Good things always make them feel inadequate and insecure. It reminded David of this girl, whom he grew up with. They called her *the kicking girl*. She was so competitive and distorted. The kicking girl played football with the boys. She fought with boys. She would beat them even though they were of the same age. The thing that was funny about the kicking girl was that she was afraid of fighting other girls, and even got beaten by girls younger than her. But with boys, there were no rules so the kicking girl always won. If you were small she would beat you, if you were bigger

162

she would kick you. She would go about provoking for fights. If you run away, then she would laugh at you so you had to stick around and fight her so that she won't have the pleasure of humiliating you. The best thing you could do was to hurl hurtful words and know they have hurt her by the way she flies at you. The kicking girl came from an unstable family.

David was still thinking of this kicking girl when Charlotte came for him. She came half an hour later and fortunately for David she was good on her word this time. She was with her friend, which he felt was a welcome thing for it meant they could try to talk to each other without trying to kill each other. He also knew that she would try to tolerate him a bit. A soft quite, a kind of soft enlacing filled David as he accompanied them to the Zengeza 2 Shopping Centre where she was going to take a lift back to Harare. Charlotte and her family had previously stayed in Chitungwiza, but later relocated as a family to Harare.

Their church, where they are meeting, was in the middle of a small forest so they took the small trail out of this forest. This small trail revolved into a footpath, which revolved into a big road. Observing this natural progression, as they were making their way, he couldn't help noticing, thinking; it should have been the case with their relationship. Even though they had been seeing the other for three years, they were still basically estranged as lovers, fighting everyday for their space and identities. Seeing her was the only thing that seemed to hem in his longing for her a bit but it also inflated his depression.

They were at the intersection of Cheuka Road and Mupini Drive when she entered the intersection without checking for traffic on Mupini Drive. David had to grab her real hard to make

163

her avoid getting run down by a truck that was coming from Mupini Drive, turning into Cheuka Road that they were in. This made him realise that there was something that was troubling her. She lightened a bit when they met some friends who were dating and the girl had a new pair of shoes. They joked with the girl telling her that her boyfriend was such a good keeper, taking care of her and Charlotte's friend, Melody, even made some jibes at David, saying that he was not doing any better by his girl. David replied her jokingly, that he was a sucker for pleasing his woman, so if he had to do something, it had to be the best there was but also that she wouldn't take it. All this was easy banter and it made them laugh a little bit and relaxes.

When they came midway their journey, Charlotte told them that she collapsed during midweek, and that she had been admitted at the Avenues Clinic, in Harare Avenues Areas, for a couple of days. He asked her what was wrong and she said, "Maybe its stress."

She looked so vulnerable with a look of exhaustion in her eyes. David would really like to hold her in his arms and protect her from whatever was troubling her but he couldn't take the chance. He asked her what was stressing her and she said petulantly.

"Dave, you could be the one who is stressing me."

It made him feel bad. He knew that's exactly how she wanted him to feel so he didn't show her that it was troubling him and that she had hurt him. David knew Charlotte liked to fight with him, and was always spoiling for a fight, and that some other times that he had avoided getting sucked into a fight with her by keeping his cool. Some other times he just couldn't keep cool but raised some of the issues with her, and they would fight it out like bloody hell.

They were just Euclidean's children, parallelism in constancy right to the end of things, and that he had come to accept that about them. He had always tried to make her feel comfortable with him but a non-Euclidean way of being in which lines, ideas, thoughts and feelings could come together here or far out there, at the vanishing Lough was not to be theirs to have. He had also come to accept that the grab zone was always too bigger and that the corners were always too sharper and that it always made her feel better whenever she had to fight things out with him. Maybe, David had just gone along, in this typical woman style, believing that if you were always fighting with your partner, then it meant there were problems, and that the relationship was doomed. He knew he believed love was not an easy chair, but it sure made the harder parts easier to work through, maybe that he just wanted the kind of love that was as comfortable as old slippers. He also knew that this fighting was corroding his sense of self worth so the only way out was for him to try to avoid situations that could put them on each other's throats

When Charlotte realised that David had ignored her, she provoked him more by saying that it would be her last time coming over to Chitungwiza, since they had finally packed as a family and were now staying in Harare. She said something like:

"There is nobody I care about good here for me to come here again."

She either was feeling the forthcoming loss to become of her move to Harare and the gravity of fear of being alone was eating

165

her consciousness, or she was really meaning well this time, that she doesn't care anymore about anyone that side of Chitungwiza.

David did not know what to say to her, but he wanted to say. "I do care a lot about you, Charlotte. So, you shouldn't be saying that." But, he couldn't say that because he was afraid it might have invoked Dear David bombs like:

"Dear David, I don't want you to care for me." "You are not so important to me, Dear David." "Dear David, I don't want your love." "Tat tat tara, tara..., yara yara yara, and Dear Davids others."

When Charlotte found out that David had ignored her again, she started to talk girls' stuff with Melody. David could only join them here and there, when he knew something about whatever they were talking of, but most of the times he was just quiet to himself. Somehow, he knew without accepting that this was going to be the last day he could ever lay his eyes on her, if she was going to stick to what she had said. He also knew that all this angst that was being directed at him had something to do with another guy she had been seeing, who hadn't been coming out good. Her friend Melody told him about this guy. Deep down David's heart, he was happy that their relationship was imploding. He was also happy that he could be the only one vying for her heart. He also made a new conviction to fight for her even though he meant to let her go when he heard about that guy a couple of weeks before. But, anyone could have realized that it was the cage that was revolving here and the bird had flown out.

By the time they reached the bus stop, they were settled into each other's company. David also knew there was something that was still bothering Charlotte. She took the next bus that came by.

166

When she was embarking and reaching for her bag that David was carrying for her, he told her he was coming with her. She was surprised but didn't protest against that. Deep down his heart, he had come to terms with the fact that this was the last time they could be seeing the other. What David wanted to do was to spend as much time with her as was possible. That's why he had instantly decided to accompany her.

She took a seat of two in the middle of the bus. When they had settled down, they started to talk of David's birth place in Nyanga, Nyatate Area. This came about when she said she still missed her time at school. This school, St Mary's Magdalene Secondary School, is in David's birth place. Even though they were now communicating well this time, he could still feel some contained thing, or some sort of energies inside her waiting to explode any moment. He also realised there was a creature inside her that he could never be good enough to bring out, or even be stronger enough to reach out for. He kept to the conversation about Nyanga. When she started to answer him with boredom yawning in her voice, he kept silent. They didn't talk about anything much after that because she was engrossed in whatever was in the storm of her heart, or in the landscape of her own psychosis. *So what gives with her?* But, he could not ask her.

Later, when he was paying their bus fares to the Conductor, she said, "This is the last time you will be paying for my bus fares, so thanks a lot, David."

She seemed to be talking to someone inside her. The conductor threw a shadow at her. She shivered, and then she stole a quick glance at him. Her emotionless icy brown eyes sending a chill- a knife of realisation through his heart, but he

167

didn't know whether it was due to fear of their parting or of something else that she was shivering. He didn't have small money to pay for their bus fares so he used the $100 billion note that he had when all that the conductor wanted was only $2 billion dollars for the two. When David gave the conductor this bill Charlotte looked at him with this look as if she was saying he was just being pretentious but the conductor told David that he would give him his change money when they would be disembarking at the Charge-Office Bus Stop.

David was dry for something more to say to Charlotte and the bus was moving so slowly as if its destination would never come and didn't even enjoy the freedom of this open road. Outside the bus, the western sky was a beautiful blue. Such sweet blue was curled around the sun, but inside the bus it was so hot, clammy, and noisy. David wondered a lot why all the other people in the bus had so much to talk to each other about when Charlotte and him didn't have anything to say to the other. This was the fitting example of the tone of their relationship for three years now. Very little to talk to each other about, and they have always been two desolate islands standing against each other, lost and abandoned. The problems they needed to fix ran deeper, leagues and leagues into the ocean of their relationship. Charlotte was very physically attractive in a fragile way. He was animated with her, but never flirtatious around her. He has always been flirty with other girls, but this lack and the dilemma was also a problem.

When they arrived at the Charge-Office Bus Stop, they were in the middle of the bus. So they followed the line of those disembarking and the queue ahead and after were ten minutes

168

long. When they disembarked the conductor still didn't have his change money, so they waited for him as he finished checking the other half of the queue of those disembarking. Charlotte started complaining about this waiting and told David that her father was waiting for her at the Fourth Street Bus Stop, so she couldn't wait any longer. David begged her not to leave him but to wait for a couple of more minutes for he still wanted to keep her company. When the conductor finished checking all the tickets he left for a couple of shops nearby to look for the change money, and this time David couldn't hold her back anymore. He let her go and she seemed like a wind, walked like it, seemed to come from it. He also realized that there were some winds he would never really understand, even though he would face them every day and that the slowness of the conductor in giving him his change money had now acted as the dominator of their destiny.

When the conductor returned back with his change money, about two minutes later, he was happy he might run and catch up with her before she had reached her father. Yet the conductor started rolling through the possibilities of numbers slowly, trying to figure out how much he owed David. At one moment, David was almost leaving everything in his anger with this conductor, but some voice deep inside him told him that he had already lost her, and that their relationship had become simply confusing, not confusing and worthwhile. That it was stupid of him to have to lose the money as well in the process. He waited through the conductor's mathematical additions and subtractions.

He didn't mind anymore how longer it could take this conductor to work through the numbers, for he was now drenched in a loss like loss he had never felt before. In the salt waters of his heart he knew that was that. She had left him with more than he had left her with. A dry sob hit his chest with the thought attached to it. *I have never really opened my heart to anyone before Charlotte. I have had a chance to do that but now she is gone.* David did not know whether he could ever find someone someday to give his heart to again. He also thought of sexual ecstasy and how he had never felt it, and of how dating- such a huge strain it was- having to gear up to acting as a social being?

When the conductor had given him his change money, he loitered through the deserted Sunday streets of this city. He was not seeing anything, even though he was sometimes gazing into the windows of the buildings in this city. His mind essaying this loitering around the city: he didn't even enjoy the falling sun's rays that he had always enjoyed before when the sun was floating low in the western skies. Its golden rays were sipping through tall and small buildings; shadows hiding behind tall buildings, and seams of sunlight escaping in gaps between them, full of confidence, laying broad healing stripes of pale gold on the gap toothed streets. All that he was seeing were the ends of these streets. He felt like the sun had cut slim wedges from its afternoon hot bakery and was throwing them out into the streets, just to make his life all the more miserable.

He just walked and walked until when he was tired, and then he took the next bus back to Chitungwiza.

POSTING THE LETTER

"You know what? Sometimes, just once in a lifetime you meet someone you care for deeply and love with every single beat of your heart. When you see them your heart tingles with beautiful music and your stomach summersaults with butterflies, and you are wordless for the sight, and you feel so warmly, so beautiful, and so alive. Oh! I will be darned if I can be able to express it any better, and instantly you know that it will never be the same again because now you can equate your life to giving out your very best." I had heard, in actual fact, I had overheard her someday, discussing with her friend, on their University prospects...I was cowardly enough, scared, such that I didn't ask her then what all that meant to us. She wanted to go to NUST (National University of Science and Technology) in Bulawayo. Maybe, I thought this was going to be something that would find its way out of her mind. 19 days later, and she was nineteen, it's when I managed to build courage to ask her whether she was really leaving me, she said.

"What else do you want me to do, John?"

I felt guilt for asking her, so I said it was Ok with me, but I didn't think it was. Not that I didn't want her to pursue her dreams...only that I wanted to be there in those dreams with her. Holding her in my arms later, I pulled her closer, describing our future on her stomach, the magnificent new world, new; that we would inhabit with her dreams. It was inevitable.

"I got a place at Midlands State University....and I am taking it, this August." We had hit July, so I knew it was a matter of time before she leaves me. When I wrote this letter, it was when she was at the University. I looked around for the address of the University and wrote to her. I wasn't even sure it would reach her. When I asked her later whether it had reached her, she said it hadn't reached her, but I thought she was lying...because once, some months later, she said I am deep, that I write things that are too deep. I hadn't written anything that had been published anywhere; I was failing to get headway on that, so the only way she could have realized that, and know that I write things that were deep was if she had seen or read the letter. It could be the following part that made her think I am deep. I was just trying to express how I felt towards her. I wasn't trying to be deep at all. Even though a little bit more of it shifted out of true, in the letter, I said,

"She touches you in a way no other woman has ever done. Touching light feels like nothing as compared to her touch, and on your own, all alone, you decide to love this stranger. You touch this stranger in your heart. You try to understand her, you accommodate her inside you, you are in her total wake, and you are straggling blue trying to tell her how you feel because the words don't come any pretty good towards perfection." Even these words were not perfect to me. I didn't think they would mean anything; something that much to her or even to me. Maybe that they could have helped me to try to understand how I felt about it all. Isn't that what we crave for, understanding.

"When you feel you can understand one or two things about it all, and when you think to yourself that you have done your entire perfect best towards having her for yourself. Suddenly you discover that the place you had nestled for her is empty. That she

172

has moved out, without a word, a gesture, a sign, nothing but silence. Silence is all that you are left with. This silence haunts you some, you feel so doomed, so desolate, so unloved and damn unworthy."

She had just left me, without telling me she was now going. I knew she might have tried to avoid a scene with me... I don't particularly like parting. I have always tried to avoid them, as well. I think it is a case of what if she might convince me, that leaving is not the best there is, would I be willing to shelve it. I wouldn't shelve it, so she didn't shelve it. She avoided a parting. Or maybe it's the angst between us, the fighting, the failure to connect...I felt that way about our relationship, she must have felt the same, too. In the letter I tried to ask her about this, whether I had made her hate me.

"Did I make you feel so bad about me? Is there anything I can do to make you like me a bit, just a little bit, and some day; love me with all the fire in your heart? I am so sorry if I made you hate me this bad, to leave me all alone without a goodbye. Only God knows I meant well, even though I might have rubbed you the wrong way. I thought, I mean in our first days of acquaintance, that you had a soft spot for me, or maybe that you might like me, but you changed. Things changed between us, inside out. I have wondered, I have often wondered what went wrong and hoped each and every day that you would find it in your heart to forgive me, to understand anything wrong that I did, I did it because I loved you." Then I borrowed a line from Dambudzo Marechera's, *The Black Insider,*

"Happiness can turn into pain..." Dambudzo was writing of a girl, the character named Barbara, whom he had dated and now

173

she didn't want to see him again. He had failed her. I felt I had failed her, as well. I didn't want her to feel guilty, so I told her not to.

"This letter is not meant to make you feel guilty because I don't have any call to make you feel anything, to ask you of anything. Ok, enough of these beget. It was meant you simply had to go. The biggest import of this letter is to let you know that it's a wonderful thing that you are now doing. Honestly, even though I would rather have you here, I would you would get the very best out of this educational endeavour. Your going away to University, your studies, throws a somewhat softer light on my wishes for I wish for a girl of great beauty and some brains. All that I am asking of you is that you keep me in your mind; you let me into your life, and not let me go." I suppose that's all that I wanted to tell her in this letter, and I have been this pell mell. The letter was longer. I did post it back then, but she said she hadn't seen it, that's why I am posting it in this book. I hope she would be able to see it this time. The other part of this letter got lost over the years. I left it with all the other stuff that I hadn't encompassed into any of the works I had back then, in 2008, when I left for South Africa. When I returned back home, in 2010, I tried to recover the stuff, but the bulk of the stuff had been lost including the rest of this letter. I have had to rewrite two stories now. I always find you don't really produce what you had back then. You can't reproduce some feelings, that's why I decided not to rewrite the parts that got lost.

"Sometimes I get to thinking of you, in a headache sort of way. Sometimes it's so painfully sweet, especially when you come unbidden into my senses, smiling so tantalisingly, so sensuously,

174

so beautifully. I would see my Jennifer Garner in you when you do that. Sometimes I remember of you laughing crazy over one of those dump jokes of mine, sometimes of your voice on the static." I have always thought when she smiles; I find Jennifer Garner in her. It just smothers me, her smiles, uncluttered.

This is another thing that you can't reproduce unless it really happened. If it really happened, you can only enjoy it, and that's what I now do. Remembering her laughing or smiling, it's been years and I feel this is a good memory for me now.

"By the way, do you still remember you had promised me you would talk to me on the Sunday you left, and now every Sunday I go to the church hoping that by the whimsies of Mother Nature's dainty, I would find you there, but I also know it's a futile hope."

So is this writing, I suppose. But I had to reproduce it, maybe it will last.

PERHAPS A PRAYER-WHEEL

And then I see her photo on the Facebook social network site, I am taken back to the day I first saw her. To the tumble of black hair curls, laughing brown eyes, and I remember of her mile long legs. She is now staring, laughing brown eyes, into my eyes. Wisps of thick black hair flows around her avocado shaped face and a blackish bluish collar of her dress fights with her hair for space around her neck. My personal control now abducted by her presence; her name is Sharon. It is now five years later. I can't see the changes time should have caused on her face. Five years have flown by since the first I saw of her, still mesmerised by her beauty, I cannot find language for even though her words were the winds that howled through all my dreams. Seeing her image on the facebook make me feel like I am still walking by her sides, we are quiet to each other. I have weathered the storm, the fight. It was about; I had phoned the wrong time and talked to her father. She is generally a shy girl, so she isn't talking that much... and I don't seem to say much as well, but we are keeping company. To my soft touches, caresses, she is stilled warm amber. Here, it's the unsaid words between us that are howling through all our dreams, prying us further apart from the other.

The sad realisation is that I have broken on the resolve I made not to phone her. I have regressed again by checking on her on the facebook, substituting phoning with this. It seems I am never meant to get out of this. Has she gotten out of this thing between us...I know I couldn't call her to ask her that now. I made the resolve not to do so. I don't intent to break on that,

176

too. To be on the safe side, I close off the facebook site, and leave for home. I am dazed…as I am walking on my way home. It is an almost blank sky above, the doors of such sky, invisible blue. It is roughly a kilometre walk to where I stay in Delville South Suburb, to the south of Germiston City Centre, in Ekurhuleni Municipality, the formerly East Rand part of Johannesburg.

For some time after I left her in Zimbabwe, I couldn't accept the fact that these old feelings that I still held in my heart for her were old lies clothing themselves in new robes. I told myself, severally, that we were done with each other. It now seems those old feelings are now like the birch and jacaranda trees along Webber Road, clothing themselves in the spring's greens. The jacaranda trees overlaps into the road, spreading their sweet shade along the small walkway besides Delville North Road where I am in now. It's October, making my mind spring; imagining photosynthesis of green leaves of January. And, the wild tulip flowers and black Susan are sprouting all over, and some blue flowers I don't know their names, especially in unkempt lawn areas along the roads in Delville South Suburb. The previous winter season, in dread I had watched the winter come, with dark shortening days, to menace my already bereft life. The few leaves on the thin branches of the trees shaking in the sudden quiet dark of the winter nights, falling off in the slate-grey air as the trees suddenly developed the heads of cancer's advanced chemotherapy treatment patients. I could have thought they were different trees to the ones I am now seeing, but they are still the same trees.

177

There is this sweet lawn covered park in Delville North Road circle. In it today, I see a couple. The girl is sitting on the swing in this park, and the boyfriend, a tall lanky handsome man in his late twenties is swinging the swing sweetly. The girl, she is a bright beautiful sunny girl, is smiling into the distances, sometimes up to her boyfriend, sometimes she is nuzzling her face against the boyfriend's hands. The trees in this park are swaying, slim columns, from the sighing winds. It's a sweet picture image. It makes me ache inside with longing, with want of Sharon's company. But, I know it is a futile longing. That world was never meant to be ours to have.

I am still smarting with longing for Sharon as I enter Menin Road, the sides of which are covered with decaying hulks of birch trees. There is this particular one. It is so old; the heart is eaten down. It's now only a small chunk about my waist's height. I know that all sorts of bugs, termites, and ants are feeding on the tree's heart. It is like my heart, I am being feasted on by things I don't have words for, in the insides. I am decaying inside my heart, decaying inside that echo place; I feel so lost... I have no one. But the tree's sides are sprouting some small brushes. These brushes are like the parasites inside the tree's heart, they are feeding on a decaying host. It's the life that this decaying trunk is giving out that amazes. I am thinking; there is always a chance, a possibility to begin again..., that's why I am thinking I have to return back home. No one wants me here.

For some time and for some years after she had broken my dreams and left me for another boyfriend, I floated in a river of denial, always telling myself that I will be fine without her. Sometimes, that I still loved her, sometimes that I don't love her

178

anymore, sometimes that I wanted her back with me, sometimes I just couldn't figure out what I wanted… And, for the last two years I have been in South Africa, I have floated in Rand's waters into its many dams, rivers, and lakes. The East Rand cities like shining beacons fleeting past me; Alberton, Germiston, Kempton Park, Springs, Benoni, Brakpan, Boksburg, Edensvale, and Edensvale; is the valley that nestles Rand's waters. I could still lie to myself that I could go on with my life without my Rand's waters. Now, I have moved far enough away from her to see the bigger picture…, the enterprise of making a dwelling place, a modest home, an honest relationship. I have come to another arrangement!

I came to this new arrangement as I was walking past the edge of a small bridge in Webber Road. I realised that I had been time-travelling, all along with panic into a world of "if only", a rebar reinforcing understanding. The views of Sharon's sweet form, this gentle longing that I still feel for her; it's a sweet world: beauty with its blunt edges now softened. Consider this story then as a prayer-wheel.

When I saw Sharon's photo on the facebook, I wanted to call her. I wanted to tell her that all I ever wanted was to be the one who would always churn her heart. I really had to tell her that. That- I would have wanted to drift into the dream of the river to the voices in her heart, but that I understand, and still do not know why she didn't want to be with me. Was it because she thought I didn't have the education she wanted, that I didn't have the kind of job she wanted her boyfriend to have, that I wasn't working, that I was not in the same social class with her, that I

179

was too old for her taking. Ten years of it must have been too much for her!

I have also wanted to call her to tell her that all I ever wanted was for her to be the whisper that appeared a moment before the words were said. That, the day I talked to her father, I really had to talk her. I had been trying to reach her on her cell phone the whole of that day but couldn't. Her cell was on voice mail, and it was a thing that drove me into craziness. Wondering why she has made herself inaccessible to me. I get to think, to obsess and, I am so jealousy. I can't even abide the thought of sharing her with anyone else, and that she might be with someone. I ended up calling her on the land line. It was slightly after 8 at night that I called her. The father, I didn't know him, I had never met him, answered me. I said to him that I wanted to talk to Sharon. He asked me what my name was. I told him, "John". He said, "John, is this the right time to be phoning?" I said,

"I am sorry sir, but I would like to talk to Sharon." He called Sharon over to the phone. As she was coming to the phone I heard her mother scolding her, calling her names, and the father joined in. They were complaining that she shouldn't let her boyfriend phone on the landline when they were home. She came to the phone and said, "What do you want?" I said,

"Hi Sharon, how are you doing?" She said she was fine, but still wanted to know what I wanted. She was so tense, taut; raged. I just said I missed her, that I have been trying to reach her throughout the day and that I just wanted to know she was fine. She cut the call. I knew it was a storm when I felt one crouching over the horizon.

180

The next day I am meeting her at the church. After church I accompany her. She is so cross with me. She shouts hurtful words at me. She tells me I am stupid.., she calls me several hurtful names. I don't like to be called names but I know I am the one wrong so I keep my cool as she works on me until her anger is sated. It is my silence that becomes a truce between us, no words from me could have held us together- would have been the root to truces between us. Now, as I get closer to the intersection of Bailluel and Menin Road, I feel I have to tell her that I was not angry with her. I was just disappointed and hurt by what happened between us. That the fights didn't end, that we kept drifting apart, and that we kept fighting and fighting...

When I saw Sharon's photo on facebook, I have wanted to call her. I told myself I would tell her that all I ever wanted was for her to clean the slate streets of my heart of the colour of this all-alone grey. This all alone grey is the colour of the grey of the tarred streets of Delville south. During the day the grey shines, flick-switch sunlight, as if it has been doused with black oil; it is a black smooth but still dirty, still inviting me to tread its streets. But, I have also learned the harder way why I mustn't tread upon a life uninvited again. So, I didn't call her.

I don't even know; would she believe me if I say that my heart still continues to surf in the swollen swell of her silence, drifting away with her? I don't know where to? I just drift and drift strung tightly in the coil of her silence. I am also learning what patience means and that it isn't always what it seems? That, the real patience eats into any silence, that it isn't afraid of silence. I now know that time standing still knowing that she is fine, without calling her to know that, is enough for me now. For years after she had left me I could just phone her to hear her voice, to hear her saying she is fine. I would call, and she would say, "Hello", briskly. I would say,

"Hello Sharon, how are you doing?" She would reply, coolly, "I am doing well, how are you doing, John." I would lie, I have to lie, and I have to sound strong; that I was over her.

"I am fine, Sharon." Then she would say,

"Say what you phoned to say, John." She is downright rude and very prudent with her time in her response like the accountant, that she is turning out to be in her career. I am still nothing, not even working, but loafing around relatives' houses. Still, I say, politely.

"I just want to know you are fine." Some fool had told me that just phoning a girl asking whether she was fine would put you in better stead with the girl, but unfortunately for me, it was raising her ire. Maybe she was different species of girls. She would then say and she is swamped in boredom,

"I said I am fine already, John." The John is dredged for emphasis, that I was boring her flat out. I would have to cut the call, I don't want her to put her boyfriend on the line again, just to spite me like she did when I insisted on talking to her, the last time when she was with her boyfriend out. So, I would say in a small defeated man's voice,

"Cool, take care, Sharon", and cut the call, but of course, she had cut the call already. I would do that for years without developing the conversation beyond that. All that I wanted was for her to talk to me, to tell me she wasn't really that displeased with me, that she didn't hate me, that, maybe, once in all those years we had known each other, that she loved me, that to love

182

her the way that I did was not a treason against her wishes… but she wouldn't talk to me. To love her, the way that I did, it seemed was treason against her wishes. But I also knew not to love her as she wanted me to do was treason against my own heart. I didn't know how to stop loving her.

And there I am, out of my day dreams, I find myself again; I am still plodding my way home, feet cracking the dry leaves, gravel and dry twigs underneath my shoes. A distracted bounce, in my steps, is hidden in the crisp particles underneath my feet. A heat-haze shimmers, a hint of amber flickers and is gone. The heat drenches me, it swelters all around me. But, I know, the air will move again even though now all that I feel is the spring's heat of mid-October swelling as if it's coming from the lawn covered sides of the road and the tarred surface of Bailluel Weg. I am at the corner of Bailluel Weg (a translator sits on my soul, want of work. Weg, this could be a slow translation of it into the air, must be the Dutch or Germany derivative of the word, street) and Menin Road. Next road is Elsburg Road, full of cars, off to Elsburg Suburb, wailing like hurt dogs; I know I am near home. We are two houses from this corner and I know that this heat drenched air will pass if the westerly wind comes from the Dugathole Squatter Settlement, to the east of Delville. The wind would set the theme; bringing in old ground accents to establish place. Dugathole Squatter Settlement is not more than five hundred metres from this lush, leafy Delville South Suburb. In Delville, you could be anywhere middle-income US suburban area. In Dugathole you are still in the larger Germiston City area.

183

It amazed me when I saw it for the first time; planks, poles, plastics, rot iron sheets for a roof over one's head; dirty, sewage, shit…unclean water, no electricity, poor people with nothing… Delville and Dugathole hugging each other was like watching two countries (Somalia and the US, maybe…) put in the same city, the known features of these countries juxtaposed by some insane painter. And, he couldn't stop painting; sometimes creating colours by mixing the greens, blacks, reds, yellows…, sometimes mixing these with shit, dirty, and sewage, and each colour becoming a section of the other colours. There is always lack of balance, a careless balance for there is no particular order in this creativity. Is this creator losing the creature, altogether, in his creativity? Walker Percy, on the "loss of the creature", said no one, can one experience a place in all its visceral reality because someone has always been there before us, has written about it, or photographed it? So, I am not going to be a laborious god-insect writer. I am not going to create anything new. Someone has already seen it before me. All that I don't know is what the creator wanted to achieve?

I also realise, it was like our relationship, the juxtaposing of the ugly and beauty. It still was like my feelings for her. I want her, I don't want her, does she love, and doesn't she love me, being contrasted from the insides of me. I still want Sharon like April's air; the way that April's air does not hold itself. I don't want her like what October air is doing right now, holding onto itself. I want her the way nothing is free enough or close enough as things in the Spar Supermarket. I don't want her like those things in Spar Supermarket. I don't want to have to buy her love for me to have her.

184

As I open the gate to our home in Bailluel Weg, I realise that seeing her photo on the facebook has broken my heart again. In the rooms, the air has that thick and undisturbed quality you would find in closed buildings whose windows have been shut, in the hot spring of October. Then, I switch the radio on, tune it a bit; I am humming silently to The Script's "Break Even" even as I rest on my bed thinking of her photo.

> *Just pray to a god that I don't believe in*
> *Coz I got time while she's got freedom*
> *Coz when heart breaks it don't break even...*

It is the song playing on Highveld Radio, at 94.7 FM, a Johannesburg radio station that I love listening to. It usually plays songs that help me deal with the isolation, loneliness, and nonentity of my existence. This is music for secluded souls that centre inwards. I am now resting on my bed from this journey from Delville Spar Supermarket. I now remember of the last summer. Last summer I made the choice of staining my house. My home is a small cottage with two rooms. The main house is owned by a relative and he allows me to use this cottage in exchange with looking after the whole place; cutting the lawns, pruning the flowers, doing the beds, etc... I have been using this cottage for a year now. It is at the back of the main house. I stained it a deep burnt caramel colour with dark red rim (burnt red) around the windows and doors. I have been holed up in this holler for a year now, filling the fitted cabins in the kitchen with odd collections and detritus.

It is a sparsely furnished home; I could even describe it as an empty home. The other furniture thing is the lovely honey-

185

grained oak table in the kitchen. The kitchen is always hidden in the shadows- sometimes dark shadows, moving deceptively, mysteriously- haunting the furniture. Occasionally, streaks of white light from the sun's rays penetrate through the slits between the blinds. The pocketed short illuminations of light are the best features of these two rooms. The colours of the rays soften my senses.

Whilst I am resting here in this tuneless silence of my life as the sound of silence of dying grass in Wyeth's painting, desire sustaining the intent to preserve this all encompassing silence, I would like to know how she has been playing my song on her heart's radio. I hope that song is David Cook's "Come back to me", or maybe Taylor Swift's "You belong with me". I have also been humming to these songs as I rest on the bed, streaming from the radio. I am thinking of her, I am listening to the radio, I am thinking of her.

I want to know whether I still stroke her with the even streams of feelings like the sweet soft sounds of the stream that divides Delville South and Delville North suburbs. Fording this meaning stream, this stream is cased under the sports ground; as it flows underneath Webber Road for a hundred metres downwards until it resurfaces again beyond Elsburg Road to the south, and then hides easily in the long whispering curtains of willow and balsam. And, in the summer, the drops of this river would swim naked in the dark haired river, in every colour, the water dancing where there was no shade. But in the winter, the water killed, and double killed by the winter's dryness is like a thief, sneaking downstream from the Rand Dam, just outside Germiston City Centre, as if it's running away from the larger waters of the dam. Maybe, it would be running away from the mournful screech of circling ducks, these water birds serenading in the water, letting out their throat corroded yells.

In this stream the water is always churning with soft key sounds; it feels like keys being softly shaken in an enclosed thing. I feel like a watery implant of her, like love; I gather beauty, tears, bubble, and flirt. And like what the river would seem to be saying to me, I am the waters in this stream. I feel like I am dozing...I am..., I must be dozing...

I am dreaming with her name. Every night, in my heart, I am always dreaming... The light I see even as I fall asleep always existing as the only call even when I know she is already asleep. She is so far away in a different country whose name is a hallow moan to me. She is smiling beautifully into the sun, at her new boyfriend like that girl in the park in Delville North Road circle. It cuts my heart into small tiny pieces. I can't seem to pick up all those small pieces of my heart, to neat them back together. I still watch her in my dreams, even at night as I call her name so that someday when we meet again, I would tell all this to her shadow. She is going; she is leaving with her new boyfriend. I keep calling for her. She is always going the different direction from me; her shadow is, as unforgiving as time! I am tripping after her. I am always tripping after her in my dreams. Telling her I needed her. She is floating away; she is flying away from me...

She is like wings of love and happiness flying away from me, an aeroplane flying on top of me from O.R.Tambo International Airport. The aeroplane is flying away to an unknown destination and this unknown destination is the way to her heart. I can't fly with her. I am earthly bound. The heavy drone of the airbus's

187

engine trembles all around the room, inside me, everywhere. I am shaken. I wake up with a start, and I look around. I am in my house, on the bed, and it is broad daylight. I am disturbed. I know I am still lost without her. I haven't mourned her enough to get her out of my system.

The Hebrews believes it takes four seasons to mourn someone but so far it has only been summer; the dark rain coming screaming horse-jets down against the horror of my face. It was summer and summer and summer..., the first year of my stay in South Africa in Kempton Park's Birchliegh North Suburb. Summer and summer and summer..., is now the second year of my stay in South Africa in Germiston's Delville South Suburb. I know without her by my side the third year will be summer and summer and summer..., the blaze of her absence in my life!

Through zones of concealment, I have walked and walked the streets of South Africa and searched for what was lost. The merit I search for is my last chance. I am at the darkest, scariest, lowest moment of my life. I know it's my fault.

It's me who have attempted to move on with my life without her, but failed. Now, I stand on a thin line.

@ THAT MOMENT

And @ that moment... *I know you really expect me to tell you when that moment was. Was it in the afternoon, morning, night? You expect the year; the moment could be a place or even it is the metafictive grip of the whole story,* I was loose cannon, firing blanks, but never refraining from it. *Okay, it was in April, the winter air was starting to speak through the door, and my worst character flaws felt so raw like the weather, an insane wind.* @ that moment I was careless with hearts, distracted from caring and remembering. *The character ran through girlfriends like toilet paper!* Not me, no! *You have to understand that the I in this story is not necessarily me, the writer.*

@ that moment I had buried my heart deep inside me. I could afford messing with others, knowing they had no way to reach mine. @ that moment I could grab anything, anyone on my paths, as long as they were willing. All these girls were soup to me. @ that moment they fell on my path like dominoes. *I have been using this word a lot, lately, dominoes. I just like the sound of it. Once I get a full taste of the idea, I forget the meanings that contained it.* @ that moment I could only pick as many as I could take in. @ that moment I was on for good time, hanging out with her, playing at being a couple. @ that moment Maud wanted more, she gave more, thinking it could make me offer more than I was offering her. @ that moment I took and took and took, never giving much back.

@ that moment we would lock ourselves in my two room lodgings, messing around. @ that moment I wasn't sure going all the way with her was the right thing to do, so I stayed put. *As a*

189

Lenten exercise, it was valuable to abstain. There is a joke told by prostitutes. Why is sex like a rumour? Because, it goes from one mouth to another or mouthhole to another, like cooked food, cooking.... *Mouths. mouthholes, cooking…it is a metaphor for…, yes that place, Vagina's open gates!* @ that moment she wanted to do it. @ that moment I was afraid of sexual related diseases. @ that moment AIDS loomed large in my sex mobbed mind, dominating it. @ that moment she would come over to my place.

One day she did, late at night. She said her parents weren't home and she wanted to sleep over. I couldn't tell her I wasn't comfortable with that, for I had never shared the night with a girl. I cooked us a beautiful meal, mackerel fish and rice. We ate it off each other's plates, sitting on the same sofa, kissing, messing... We couldn't finish eating properly as we were all over each other. We kissed and kissed until it hurt our teeth. We touched and touched. Maud sat on my legs striding me, kissing me down, until I could only keep my mouth open. We ripped each other's clothes. Throwing our clothes all over the room, some on top of the food we had been eating. She kissed me down, licking me like a lollipop. She took me into her hands and started jerking me dry with her long nailed fingers, cutting into the soft skin of my molar. The pain jarred me out of the passionate world I had been in. I couldn't take it anymore, so I shrugged her off me, put on my pants and told her I wanted to sleep early. She pouted and told me she was just trying to make me happy. That she had read about it in Playboy magazine. I told her it was painful and that I couldn't, wouldn't, come on with pain. She told me to jerk myself off next time. She put on her clothes and asked me to take her to the taxis.

190

@ that moment I wished I could hold her back and spent the rest of the night with me, not for the courage she had shown. *Not for this pimped out pornographic bleached blonde silicon saturation bubonic sickness but for sweet cotton caressing tender touch titillating, wisely waiting climax.* @ that moment I regretted I hadn't taken her, all those instances she had offered herself to me. *Later, I took care of myself, down there, when she had gone. It felt like I was smoothening out of me the kernel that makes me a person.* @ that moment I knew we would never come back to that point again. @ that moment she started avoiding me, telling me she was busy with something else. @ that moment I learned how to let her go. @ that moment we drifted badly, as she moved in with another guy. @ that moment I was with another girl.

@ that moment, I always return back to that moment she tried to give me a blowjob, and wonder is the new guy benefiting from what my spanning off of her might have knowledged her with. @ that moment I would watch their photo on *WhatsApp*, they seemed *soooo* happy, and it would make me wonder if I should have made us last, and teach her how to give me a pleasure mobbed blowjob. I once asked her about us. She said, she swore, she doesn't remember she loved me, even though I could draw out of her sword-like pleasure howls, off her breasts as I kissed her breasts, whilst the wolves outside wept in pleasure, too. *There is not much to make of it. We might supply our own meanings here. It depends upon our tenuous connections to the grand scheme of things. We don't know what it is, maybe we know, but we might be the poorer for the lack of it.* @ that moment I could have asked her to cut down her nails, lotion her hands before working on me. @ that

191

moment I could have enjoyed it, better. *But now a sentence that approximates forgiveness (that, "I am sorry") will have no start or terminus!*

Shutting out all of the hearts that bleed for you is a mistake. I am clever enough to know that now.

COLLEEN

I have been watching her like a hawk, for most of the year. I didn't know why...but my eyes would find their way to Colleen's direction. She seemed calm, sweet, that kind of silent beauty that's slowly stoking and fascinating. It's easy to get absorbed into this kind of beauty because you don't really know you are getting absorbed. It is like the way the sponge soaks water, how I was getting soaked into her. It's not intense or demanding. It is a soft, a soft butterfly's take. And then, I started wanting to talk to her. I would try to figure out how, or just find something interesting to say to her, or even at that, to begin with, just finding myself near her. I knew she knew I had been watching her, so she would come close to me. She would spend some moments near me. Sometimes we would exchange pleasantries; sometimes we would just hang along, that feelingly good hanging together. It was easier to hang around her. After all she is not demanding or intense. I didn't tell myself I was really interested....even though I knew deep down that I was getting interested. It's easy to depend on meaningless conversations in situations like these.

"Could I join you in your umbrella on your way home, Colleen?"

It was raining that day, a Sunday afternoon, somewhere in March. It was now three months since I had started noticing her. Umbrellas have always fascinated me since Rihanna popularised them with her song, Umbrella. "Under my umbrella ella ella e e e eh...," the sensuous Rihanna, sizzling beautiful, step dancing like a lark in March's rains, in the video of the song. It's a sensuous

193

world to be inside an umbrella with a girl you like... Your shoulders constantly brushing and it is raining a sweet, sweet March bubbling misty rain... It's even more beautiful when she is the one you love...you are holding her hands or hugging each other or your hand is holding softly onto the small of her back...

"Yes, you can join me, Tawanda", she replied me.

But we lived in different directions, I realised that when she said she stayed in Zengeza 4. I am going the opposite direction, to Zengeza 1 where I stay. The church is in Zengeza 3, so how could it be possible for me to share with her an umbrella to her home? There is no ways she is going to let me go with the umbrella to my place, maybe for the rest of this week, until we meet again the next Sunday. But I just wanted to be under her umbrella with her. She balked a bit later when she realised I was serious...and maybe, what all that really meant.

"But, I have someone else I am sharing the umbrella with, Tawanda. We also go the different directions from here", she said.

I could only get glum. It's not a boy she is sharing the umbrella with so I am still hopeful. I couldn't even tell her it is just a ploy, an unconscious ploy, maybe conscious, to hold on to her. She must have figured out that.

Then there were some months after that when we could just hang along, here and there, besides I had other things on my mind; another girl I was still pursuing. I did let things drift along, showing her that I liked being with her. She would approach me, hang with me, and still she wasn't demanding. Was I falling for her? I didn't even explore things that far. I had become used to discovering that once I name something, most likely it would

194

always find a way to unnamed itself, to undefine itself, or to even elude me. So I don't. I just let things be as they are. As I realised things with this other girl I had been courting were imploding I was tending to think a whole lot about Colleen. I was thinking I should be making more of effort to tack things with her, but I still took my time. At least six months after beginning to get into her, I started pushing things a bit more. I started telling her I wanted to be with her. I really wanted to be with Colleen. I really did started seeking her. Colleen realised things had changed between us, somehow. She realised this as she would hang quite a lot more with me. For some weeks on end I told her I wanted to tell her something, that I wanted to spend some more time with her, and that I wanted to get to know her a lot more. For some time I didn't know what I really wanted to say to her. I had always thought saying that, "I love you", to a girl is a bit kinky, especially when you don't really know what all that you are feeling inside you really means. I knew I liked Colleen, I knew I was attracted to her; I knew I wanted to spent some more time with her. I didn't want to call that love, yet. So, I skirted around this, but there is a time I started saying those words I love you to her without feeling there were not really there in the right sort of way. I would say that, and I would repeat it again, and felt I needed to keep saying it, so I would always find a way to say it. What we say has always a way to find its way into making itself the truth, especially to us, even though sometimes, it will not be a shared truth. It did. Slowly, I began to find I was feeling things, I was falling in love with her.

It's one thing to say I love you to a girl, and another to realise you are really falling in love with her. It sometimes scares the hell

195

a lot but somehow you have to find your feet and stand on your legs or else you will lose yourself into the girl. You need to really figure out what she is thinking about it all. I asked her about all that, and she said,

"I am with someone. I am getting married next August".

It is a year from now, I tell myself as the implications of this sunk into my mind. It is like being hit by a large ocean wave. I was stunned, I felt stunted. For a moment I didn't know what to say. If I wasn't into her in a big way, I could have shrugged my shoulders and said,

"So what?"

But I knew I needed to delve deep to find what truthfully that really means to me, or even to her. Then Colleen gave me a bit of light to see things a lot bit clearer. I couldn't call it hope. It was a lot too little to call it that.

"In fact, my boyfriend wanted to marry me this December, but I refused", and I asked her

"Why not?"

"We have problems. I wanted him to solve something..."

"What something?" I couldn't let go of this light. I wanted it to shine my way through this already fouled up feelings world of mine. It's like I have just realised I am in love with her as she is rejecting me!

"I asked him to relocate to around here. He works somewhere in Marondera Town. I want him around here before I could commit to him."

It gave me strength as I said:

"If you refused to get married to him this December it means there are deeper problems than you are letting out, Colleen."

196

I also wanted to tell her distance doesn't really matter. That the boyfriend is 75 km away is a non-event. It is a non-event for some people, but I couldn't say that because I knew it was such a huge event. I have terribly failed to sustain a long distance relationship all my life. Who was I to say that to her? I have my own insecurities, doubts and fears, and there are usually brought to the surface when I don't know what a partner is doing, is thinking of; where she is, what world she is inhabiting different from my own. I usually tell myself I live my life without all these doubts and insecurities. It's a lie I tell myself. I would lie to myself that insecurities, doubts and fears don't really affect me, especially when it is a close relationship, and when she lives close by. In these instances, I let go of all fears, doubts and insecurities and live my life without these. I just follow my heart. I wanted to tell Colleen she should do the same, but I didn't, as she said feelingly.

"All I am looking for is someone who truly loves me."

I love you, don't you see that, but I couldn't tell her that, yet the word love floating between us, bubbling in letters, the word sounded happy, almost drunken. It was a daisy chain hung around the neck of a child.

Love is always around us. We have to open our eyes to find it, I couldn't say that, as well.

Or even,

We have to open our hearts to embrace it when it calls for us.

Because I knew all that would sound like a well rehearsed joke being explained? For we are always made to think we have to go out there looking for, hunting for love, other than going deeper inside ourselves to find us, our hearts, and to create an open environment that would allow love to find a base inside us.

Things like that; you can't explain them to a girl. You want the girl to figure out that on her own. It's difficult having to take such a stand, as well. For it is a lot easier to just butt in and tell the girl what to do. I didn't want to do that, I didn't want her to think I was lecturing her. I didn't want to be a teacher. I have always fought against being a teacher, or a role model. You create some expectations that you might fail to fulfil on and, you don't want that to stay on your conscience. So, I let all that range inside me. I leave her alone to find her way.

The problem is they always might get lost. Lately I had begun to think she was getting lost to me. When I am losing out on a girl I tend to enjoy, or crave for, like sweets, pain or art forms that deal with broken heartedness, pain, suffering etc... And as I am thinking of her I am also listening to music from Chris Doughtry, Blue October, David Cook, Avril Lavigne... but, I am not hurting a lot this time. Maybe I have grown used to dealing with these feelings, or maybe I am simply more mature, and can deal with pain in a little less painful way. So that, it's Doughtry's song that I am mostly repeat playing, Tennessee line. Doughtry is saying he found himself again. Did he visit Tennessee from his LA base? Tennessee is the home of Country music, to find himself he had to delve into this American folk music genre that originated in the southern states of the USA, or rural Canada. I love Country music. I am always transported into the simpleness of life, love, living..., with this type of music. One would learn to give, take, forget, forgive, and that's what Doughtry is saying. He is saying he started living without doubts. That, it's his heart he will follow this time around, in his way to find his path home. He is following the Tennessee line.

Doughtry's music is a sweet, sweet clanging, sometimes cutting; rock music with that Tennessee's Country music feel. It is about finding your way home. It's about following your heart; it's about living without fear and doubt; insecurities. It's all this I wanted to tell Colleen. That it doesn't really matter that she is with someone, that he has promised to marry her next August, and that she doesn't want to hurt him. All that matters is she should find her way to her home. It's a place inside her that makes her feel fulfilled with herself; loved, wanted, desired. It's her who has to make this journey. She might as well go alone. Not with me, not with the said boyfriend. If she really wants to find love it should really be about her. If she wants to be happy she has to be truthful to her inner impulses, and follow the path those inner impulses are telling her to follow. She has to find her own Tennessee line. I couldn't tell her all that because our world was muddied.

She is getting lost to me. And I feel like I have been tripping after her and I don't want to be doing that. So the best I can do now is to let Colleen find herself, to follow the path she deems right, even though that path might exclude me. If she realises she wants to be with me she would have to find her way to this home. This is what I believe in. This is where I am with her. I can't push her any further than I have done. I only hope she will find her path to her home, and that I am that home for her.

I am nestled in ready for her.

199

AGE HAS NO NUMBERS?

I have always thought and I still feel that it's difficult to write love stories. They are some love stories that I feel, even if I were to manage to write something down about them whatever I could have written couldn't have expressed much about those stories. Only through bleeding, only through burning into ash and only through my death could these stories be expressed. All that I could do was to try to say my story without going through to these extremities and this is one of those love stories.

Sometime in April, 2004, we were organising for a fundraising activity, St. Vincent fundraising at my local parish St. Agnes Catholic Church. This was a youth outreach program to the community, and we were raising money to feed the poor of our parish. I was the Vice-Chairman of the fundraising committee for this function and in the same committee was this sweet, sweet girl. The first day I saw her, we were having our first meeting, outside the church, in the sun, on the church lawns. I said "hello" to her. She said "hello" to me back, smiling sweetly. With a shaft of sheer male appreciation, I took in her tumble of black hair curls, laughing brown eyes, and mile long legs encased in black tights beneath a short cherry-red skirt. This enticing combination made me almost mad. Oh, Sharon (that's not her actual name) was so sweet. Aren't they all sweet in the beginning! Yes, this child woman was so full of sparrows, but it was her sweetness and her tall curvy figure that crucified me straight away.

I didn't know Sharon for she was coming from another youth group St. Agnes and Alois youth group. I was from St. Simon Peter and Maria youth group. It was not a given that I would know every other youth at this church unless of course there were in the same group with me. So, when I came to know about

200

Sharon, it was when we made this same committee. We also came to talk and sometimes just acted polite and sweet to each other. Isn't that how trouble always starts? It was Sharon's child-like laughter and beautiful smile that I became instantly aware of and everything got to revolve around her. Down side of this I hated it. I really do hate it for I want to have a little bit of power. Strangely, it is power play that's more interesting in a relationship. You wonder what a relationship is, I know. But that's what I would have preferred.

It's like I would be a disciple of some sort to these love-mad activities pining for redemption and for heaven from the outside because I know that from the inside, it was too good for me. I am sorry I prefer to be a tourist here, holding the object of love from the outside than being a pilgrim because I know being a pilgrim could only result in me getting hurt. But, when you have to spent a lot of time together with this object of your love, this uninvolved posture melts away easily because she becomes more human, more like the girl next door, so that you would get to have a little bit of confidence to look directly at this image of all the things that you have always wanted your ideal woman to have. This lack of space doesn't bother you anymore; you don't become annoyed, or fall into silence as you used to do with other girls.

You don't only pray to this girl. You also believe in her, especially when you were with her. Maybe when she is smiling sweetly at you, or her eyes are focused on you, she is attentive to you. She blushes, when you lock eyes with her. You feel like you could just hold her in your arms and absorb her into your being so that she would always be there in you whenever you breathe, smile, laugh, sleep, eat or do everything else. When you are with her, you also lose your sense of large, ambiguous things. I think a

201

lot of it is just pure infatuation, and whoever said infatuation is not love?

Sharon would avoid all the other guys at this church who were some hissing bees after her nectar. She would come over to me and hang out with me even before I had plucked enough courage to tell her that I was some crazy-lots about her. You should know how this made me feel like.

For a couple of weeks or a month or so after I had told Sharon about my feelings, I hit the roof. Loving her to distraction, I was in irretrievable land. It felt good to be me, to have this, and to see how it was coming together. It took the two of us to push the relationship into place. This feeling filled me with confidence. Little did I know that this dream could easily be conflated by the process of making ordinary human interchanges and conflicts and that we would grow more and more apart and estranged?

I had so much to tell her when I knew I would be meeting her. When we got together, though, I said very little. Most of the times, we were just silent, not a probing silence but just good silence, but still kept company of the other. I should have tried harder to be more verbal. I suppose it could have helped me unlock her. Talking in a relationship is good because you can get to tell her about how you feel in other words other than the "I love you" phraseology every time. Maybe, if I had talked to her more about myself, then I could really have encouraged her to talk a little bit more about herself too. But, I had no words for the way I felt. I still do not have words for that.

I also wanted her to feel that I am not going to break everything up, that it would be safe for her to pick up a crate of eggs or a glass of wine. So, all that I did was to say, I love you, I love you, I love you. That's the best I could express how I felt. I literally experienced withdrawal when I was away from Sharon. I

202

was dead inside until I got another fix of her again. It was a prayer situation, the situation I was in; believing that she instinctually knows the things that I couldn't tell her. Just as a prayer doesn't say all that we want our God to know, yet he knows all that we really want, all that we are asking of him. In most cases, we don't even know what to tell God, the right words but he knows. After all, she was my god!

Sharon was nineteen, so beautiful and fragile. So unpredictable! They are like that at this age, aren't they? Yes, they still want to be teenagers, but confuse the world with their maturity. The thing is that they are just girls trying to be women, what they know of a woman. I am sorry for this sarcasm, but this is the truth: there are too hot to handle at this age. I was thirty then. The number thirty; has its own magical contents and complexities, but that depends on the person. But nineteen, like a villanelle consisting of nineteen lines, five tarcets and one concluding quatrain, is nineteen. Enough of this, juxtaposing people with age for age has no numbers, they say and I agree. Even though now I am in my middle thirties, I still feel so young at heart. I agree, like I have said, that age has no numbers, but it wasn't like that with her.

I knew Sharon was interested in knowing how old I was, but for some time she had no courage to ask me about that. She even asked her best friend, Lorraine, to ask me about my age on her behalf, but I told Lorraine,

"No, no, friend, we don't do it that way."

If Sharon was interested in knowing my age, then she had to ask herself. Lorraine understood. Eventually, Sharon plucked enough courage to ask me. I told her I was thirty that year. Instantly everything changed, or seemed to have changed. She started to bicker badly about our ages and age differences.

"You are too old to be my father, John." She would say, over and over again. This nettled me.

"How could she dare compare me with her father when she was just about ten years younger than me?" But, like some bloody shrew, Sharon began to use this as a sticking point in whatever disagreements we had. She would say, cruelly,

"You will die and leave me a widow." She also began to tear into my flesh and each time the healing would take a bit longer. Her blows were going deeper and deeper into my soul. I fought her like hell, too. Sometimes I would ask her,

"How do you know you won't die before me, Sharon?" Like I said I don't believe in numbers and here she was trying to define all that I felt for her by quantifying it into numbers. Of course I couldn't have had it that way, so I fought her.

The more we fought over this, the more the aura of our magical land became the grotesque limbo land of Edward Burra's paintings. Our barbed-wire voices tangled at every space. Even when there was really nothing to say to each other, we always found something to say just to hurt the other. The weight of this knowledge, pushing a cracked spine such that by the time she left for university studies in Gweru in September of that same year, I was just holding onto one string that she would eventually come around some day and accept me for who I was, not for my age. The truth is that and, I would like to set it out now, Sharon never told me; in all the years we were seeing each other that she loved me. It's not a huge thing that she didn't, for not a lot of girls can say that to a guy, especially shy young girls. A boy sometimes just looks for signs. If a girl is willing to spend a lot of time with you, then that's already a beginning. Even though I could see glimpses of things in her eyes, Sharon couldn't quite bring herself to shoot me with her eye's soft voice of love, no. Yet, I badly wanted to hear those words, at least just once. A man sometimes wants to hear those words!

Sharon left for Gweru, 300kms away from Chitungwiza. On her part, I think, she started drifting apart, but I couldn't have entertained that thought because she had once promised me that one day she would tell me about her feelings for me. My job was to continue cultivating this patch of land and take good care of it, so that someday in the future, I could have good harvests out of it. I didn't give up so I kept phoning her, sometimes more than once a day, sometimes I would text her some sweet and cool messages. When she came back for the holidays, I was there for her. Time activated and flew away on this hoping-for-the-best out of the relationship.

Two years down the line, she returned back to stay in Chitungwiza and later in Harare and she was now doing her year of industrial attachments at a firm in Harare. Even though I still was pushing for my cause, I discovered that things had taken another swerve with her, that we had made the curve as if it wasn't there and trundled along the silence of that road. Like a long-sought-after-road-to-the-heavens, there was still a window, a brief window here and there and a love already anticipating its own absence. Beneath all that, we were still trying to make things work out by building some shrine of some sort to everything that was already lacking by measuring our love against time lost being together. As long as it was one or two degrees closer to what could be endured, it sufficed enough for us to be there for a little while for the other. But, like a beautiful coil, our love continued to rise to the heavens as a never-ending dream until what had gone out into the skies was all of our love and soon was forgotten, leaving a cell-block cage crammed with our long tossed-away time.

205

When we are in such life or love-embodied affairs, it's not easy to come to terms with that and we take a lot of time making excuses as to why things have turned out this bad with our adored subjects. I think it is us trying to go through this unpleasant circumstance without hurting too much. By the end of that third year and by the end of that year of her industrial attachment, deep down my heart, I knew that there was now very little between us, that somehow I had lost Sharon over the years. I can't still say when I lost her. I think it would be impossible to say when for it is a matter of the heart. Can anyone tell his heart that it shouldn't be feeling the things it is still feeling when it is feeling the things it is feeling. There is neither top nor bottom of the world, neither an end to eastwards or to the westwards, only the way your heart accepts as best. One has to wait until the inner system has dealt with failure of a relationship to have real closure. I wish I can be more rational about it and do some mathematical combinations and permutations to solve this complex number problem just to confirm that her departure really was because of the numbers only. The truth is that and I was so stupid not to think about it, she was still growing up and growing up has its own pressures, its own permutations and combinations. Nineteen is the time when you start panning out and nobody controls the outcome, not even love. It's an out-of-life experience that you would be going through when you are nineteen. One can only hope that when they come out of the growth, they would still want to be with us. Deep down, that's what I pinned for.

She came out differently. She didn't want to be with me anymore. I still wanted her. The truth is that you can't force yourself into that mixture. I am so sorry that I couldn't just kill myself so that I could get out of this land. I am stuck in this land like a pig stuck in its own faecal. I can only hum along to David Archuleta's "All I want is you" as I write this story.

206

Yes, the years may have passed by. Yes, she is still be catching my eye. Yes, she is still improving... with age like old wine, they say. Yes, I love who she is now. What is that? The truth is that she doesn't want you, yet you want her. It's nice to say those words on a piece of paper, but try to write them in your heart. Will them into your heart, then you will get to know it's another thing altogether.

It doesn't happen for you!

What still beats the hell out of me is despite my love for her, I lost her. Sharon is human, I know that. Doubt is the scourge of our everyday life and she is not an exception. Yes, she could have doubted how I felt for her some other times. It is like that, shit happens! But she also came to a conclusion that what I felt for her was not good enough. This thought still boggles me. She must have known that she had me at her fingertips and only a thumb of her fingers could have brought me to her, in whatever mode of form she wanted me to be. But I didn't know who she wanted me to be and nobody could tell me. I could have sung her favourite songs for her, become Justin Timberlake or P-square. If she wanted me to be Brad Pitt, I could have become Brad for her. If she wanted, then she and I could even have adopted a United Nations family of her whims, whines, feelings or even misbegotten ideas. But the truth is that she just didn't want to be with me.

Maybe, it could be this in-your-face attitude that I took with her by pestering her about us through phoning her, through creating situations in which we had to meet that kept us on the drift, all the more and the thin air of her heart kept gobbling us and punting me out. Maybe, I should have left the relationship when there were many hints lingering around her: university studies, age differences, avoidance, and rejection. When my mind told me to take a hike, I did not because my heart wasn't ready for departure.

This was how the road was like to me. I loved, cried, laughed, believed, and got hurt. Pain and happiness intertwined and became the normal way of my life for five years. I could only kill her or she could only kill me and killing me was the only thing that I could do. It was the only thing that I had courage for.

Four years later, I left Zimbabwe for South Africa. Perhaps I had the dream of escaping the complexities of this relationship as the intervals between one's goings and comings sever the years as a hyphen severs the flow of a sentence. Yet, a couple of months after my departure, I was phoning Sharon already. She started being nice to me on the phone and asked for some money, a couple of times. She was such a sucker to think that she could scrounge money from me that easily because I loved her. I promised her that I would be sending her some, but I never did and never will. The reason is, to begin with, I didn't have the money to send to her. Even if I had some, I knew I would never have done that. Sharon had lately been treating me as a second hand boyfriend, before I left for South Africa. She had never really wanted me in her life, and why the bloody hell did she think I could just sent her money on such a silver plate? For goodness sake, I am not a bank. Had she shown or told me that she was wrong about how she treated me all those years? That, she now wanted things to work out between us and, if she had given me a little bit to grab and hold onto, maybe I'd buy into it and could have given her the money she was asking for.

I could have borrowed money from somebody to send it over to her if I wanted to. You may think that I am stingy. Sure, money is not such a big deal. Money should be shared with loved ones. It is just a bunch of numbers. One thousand dollars is one thousand numbers of dollars, so was my age to her. Remember

208

that! I don't care that much about the money. All I care is that I have just enough of it to get me by. I will throw every penny in if I can help ones I deeply care for any day. This time, it's about my feelings. I don't have any intention to let my feelings get played by anyone. I will do some serious emotional budgeting. It's just so unfortunate that she still couldn't figure out how much I really loved her after all these years of my devotion towards her!

As we started talking again, she encouraged me to return for the Christmas holiday. Although I thought it was still too early to return back, I was sort of enticed by the suggestion. Contemplating with the suggestion, I asked her one day if she would see me when I go back home. She categorically said no! Afterwards, I stopped phoning her and drifted for another six months. When I phoned her again, she was angry with me because I hadn't been phoning her.

This has always been difficult for me to process; why Sharon would complain if I stopped phoning her and that when I kept in touch with her, all she could do was to make it such a painful experience for me by bickering and fighting me all the time. Maybe, it was her habit towards people; she once said that she was difficult to deal with? I would always feel like I am in an emotional rollercoaster when I am with her. It's like you love someone deeply, but she says she doesn't love you and wants you to go. Of course, when you try to go, she would complain that you shouldn't have tried to go. The next day, when you phone her again, she would tell you that she really like you to go and leave her alone.

Since the last talk on the phone with Sharon, it has been hell for me. I made my best effort not to call her. Every day, I fight this urge to log her numbers onto my cell phone and press the dial button. Anyone who has gone through a drug experience would understand what I am talking about here and how difficult

209

it is to get over the temptation. There are times when I tried to close off my mind and stop thinking of her, hoping that pain will be minimised.

At least, I am far removed from her. There is no possibility that we might meet in the streets. All that I can do is to fight this urge to phone her. I am not saying that it's easy or I am succeeding, no. I am not even saying it is helping that much either for healing this wound because she is all that I still think of, if I think of anyone at all. She is all that I have thought of all these years even when I lied to myself that I was over her and that I am now in love with this other girl whom I would be dating, but a couple of days, weeks, or even some months later, I might start calling Sharon again.

This is what I have been dealing with. I am now tired of lying to myself and to these girls. For this past year or so I haven't looked at any other woman because I didn't want to waste their time. I am going to remain faithful alone for as long as it takes. I want to prove to Sharon that moving on is possible, if I stay faithful to the idea. But, it is still only when I am thinking of her that I feel complete. It's only when I am thinking of her when I feel my heart in my chest. It's only when I am thinking of her, frozen in time squares, that I feel complete. I still want all these feelings boxed up by their own magic without my having to touch any of it or the things in it. This is the hardest part: to let her go.

I will try to stay away from her if that's what I have to do for the rest of my life. I won't try to call her. I will try everyday not to even think of her if that's what I have to do so as not to complicate my situation all over again. Maybe, I will be successful. Maybe, I have been mentally preparing my mind for this. I am not promising myself that I would always be successful. It is my mind and heart that I don't know what to do with. I can

210

deal with my mind during the day. It's my heart I don't have a clue on.

My heart is a different genre altogether. It is a trip hammer thumping every second and its beat is louder and louder, twenty four hours a day, seven days a week, fifty two weeks a year, year after year. Every muscle in my heart, every iota in my heart, every vein in my heart, and every ounce of blood in my heart chime a song, Sharon. Perhaps, we just weren't meant to get out of this!

So, who is going to monkey-wrench us out of this ruin?

RUNNING AWAY FROM THE LOTUS POSITION

I am running harder and harder, it's a cliff I am ascending. It is a very long cliff. The way down from this cliff has been enjoyable. I didn't have to put a lot of effort. It's always easy to say you are going running, long distance running. The school, Marist Nyanga, where I am an A level student, is just below the Nyanga range of mountains, so that running back to this school is running up the cliff. That's the hardest part of this long distance running for me. Twenty years later, I am on the floor, hard on my bum. I am in a lotus position. My knees are like corkscrews, the soles of both feet point roughly to the skies, giving thanks to the powers above. I am saying a mantra in Sanskrit, Om mani padmi hum. Why don't I say it in English or Shona? Om mani padmi hum, are there no Shona translations for this? For goodness sake we are in Zimbabwe, not India. I don't even know what they mean.

In the lotus position, I am reminded of twenty years ago. Running was something that was cool with my gang then, the school-going chums. Lotus is what is cool with my midlife chums, and that's why I am trying to find my position. Back then, even when I was running 6 plus miles from the school down to the junction on Nyanga road, and back to the school, I didn't still like it. But I was trying to create community with the cool kids. I never liked running, in general. Why bother. I would never be an accomplished runner like Tendai Chimusasa, Abel Chimukoko, Haile Gebre Selassie...no, I will never. But, I would still do it during every sports hour. I was doing this, I had been told, to gain fitness, physical fitness.

Now, I am doing this lotus to gain wisdom. Who said you have to turn yourself into a plant, or into a plant's posture to be wise. Are plants any wiser than us? The instructor told me wisdom comes from making the mind totally blank. Do plants have blank minds? Isn't a dead person supposed to be blank minded? Free from what, I asked her. From intrusive thoughts, unmuddied by flash floods of emotions, she said. But I didn't know how I could empty my mind. I suppose I could empty it the way we empty our bins on Tuesdays. But, it is the smell that stays, and a hallow place where the dirty was. Is that empty? Om mani padmi hum, is it the same as hiha, hiha, hiha, punting out steam, dirty, shit... My body glistens in sweat. I can barely hold my breath, only emptying it out concurrently with the, ha, in hiha chants. Every muscle in my body is stretched.

I was told that after every run, when the body has cooled down, I would find peace, relaxation, improved digestion, and a joyous merging of the Cosmic energies in me. Om mani padmi hum, the instructor is telling me the same now. The extra benefits, she says, is it would cure my backaches, and any other aches. Om mani padmi hum, but it is creating some new aches, all over my body, my knees and feet are full of tremors, of aches. My being is becoming blank, my mind must becoming blank. My feelings are on the lower simmer, the floor is harder and harder on my bum.

It starts with believing. When you believe in it, you don't think of anything else, thus you get into this blank world. So, I tell myself- I believe I could reach peace of mind. I have the very best of instructors, a black belt welding instructor, a Zen roshi. Rice? It reminds me of rice fields in the south East Asian' sweltering, waterlogged lands, but this Roshi is an African princess. She is powerful and she carries a bamboo stick, and walks around softly- like a cougar. Om mani padmi hum, hiha, hiha, hiha.

213

I remember, one of my primary school teachers, Nyamavhuvhu. He was also our sports master. He was a cruel lion. He was a bastard of the first order. He carried the unfurled, pointed thorny part of a strong fibre stem, behind us when we were running. If you were to be caught by him, he would bore your bum with this strong thorn, and it would pain like hell. My bum feels like that now. The floor is harder into me like those fibre thorns of Nyamavhuvhu. But you would cry out in pain, back then, and bolt at a high speed, away from, WHACK!, the bamboo stick. It hits me on my back. I blink harder, shake my head, and then try to concentrate on the lotus, on my mind. Om mani padmi hum. The bamboo stick, just like the thorn fibre, has prevented me from backsliding.

I am chanting, Om mani padmi hum, Om mani padmi hum, Om mani padmi hum, fervently. Why am I bothering taking this run, this lotus position? Ideas, intrusive, start spinning in me like Catherine's wheels. Who has said the body has to be exercised? Who said the mind should be exercised? Why? I can barely raise my legs- but I am still a kilometre away from the school. I could just let it go, walk a bit, cool down. My heart is on fire- I feel blood in my nose, in my head. My mind seems mixed up with hot blood, broiling steaming-hot water, it is a burning mind. I have since stopped the hiha, hiha, hiha chants, as I climbed the foothill, Mount Love. I don't have extra energy for that, anymore. The gravel road makes it so difficult for my footing. The road is too heavy.

Imagine yourself. There you are, a simple peasant, seeking enlightenment. After a barefoot walk across the foothills of the Himalayas, in the snow, you arrive at the appointed (who appointed it?) Bo tree. You are the Buddha, in a session now. So that, after three hours of it, you open up your blank mind, and then you clear your throat- nothing is quiet. Birds are all over

214

exploding in song, in the trees, the caw and roar of the bears, the wind whistling... This isn't quietness, WHACK!

Om mani padmi hum, Om mani padmi hum, I am trying again. Hiha, hiha, hiha, I have found my voice again. I have cleared away Mount Love, but it is still steep running. I am urging towards school. I know I would make it. It is just three hundred metres away. I know I would just bowl over in the grass, by the dorms, cool off a bit, get a nice drink, sip it with other cool kids, and talk about the run as if I had accomplished something worth the chatter. What?

Then, I would have my bath, and then go for the evening studies. It's just 45 minutes of evening study, but I hate it. It is so taxing to get through that, because one is anxious to discover what's beyond that. It would be supper, at six. Today it's a Friday, so it is my favourite dish- Sadza and chicken. The other days, it's always Sadza with beans, milk, beef, or worse with plain vegetables. My mouth waters, WHACK!

Om mani padmi hum, thank you Master, Mistress, I don't remember. But we are supposed to thank them for every bamboo connection with our flesh. There is no easy walk to enlightment. My mind is full of pain. It is not blank, it is not blank, but it is now wiser. Doesn't pain and chaos make the mind wiser? It is the pain of hunger that has consumed me. I look around the room. All the other meditators are sitting in a lotus position, eyes closed. I suppose, their minds are full of nothing. Mine is full of hungry pains. I can't concentrate when I am hungry. I would stop doing any work when I was hungry. I would stop ploughing the fields. I would unyoke the cattle, and sleep off, or meditate the hunger off. Until someone who is cooking our meals comes with something to eat, I wouldn't wake up from this sleep. I would be so angry, so miserable, my mind so full of hunger. Nobody would talk to me. I would beat them if they tried. I would concentrate on my mind.

Now, older, I know what to do. You learn how to channel the hunger and anger with age, to make decisions without always resorting to violence and brinkmanship. The Roshi is gazing out the window, Om mani padmi hum. My back is sore, my bum is numb, my feet are upsides down, and my entire mind is burning in hunger. I am still running harder, though. There is only some fifty metres to the grass, but it seems the longest fifty metres, I have ever run. Inch by inch, millimetre by millimetre, I am crawling, in my lotus position towards the door. Om mani padmi hum, must mean, running away from the lotus position. What else would it mean? Nobody is noticing me, not even the Roshi, who is absorbed with the outsides. Inch by inch, I am getting there…, everything is darker and darker. My head is a cauldron of dark hot energy, and my chest is a blast furnace. Will I ever feel my knees again, my back, my feet?

I am still crawling in my lotus position. I hit the steps on the doors, and just tumble onto the walking path outside. There is screeching, whistling, and beeping of car horns, the steady hum of people passing by. I have unscrewed myself from the lotus position. I am up and bolting away as the Roshi's bamboo stick tries to connect. I am running harder even as I pain, like hell. My friends are off at the chicken place, I know. I am off to the corner of George Silunduka and Innez Terrence Street. There is a big chicken place there.

A moment later, here I am in the Chicken Inn, on my chicken-eating position, consuming a chicken burger with chips and coke. We are talking with my friends about the 6 mile run. Running from what? The lotus position? The chicken burger is really good. Om mani padmi hum. The chicken is good hahi, no, its hiha, hiha, hiha. Who cares, really? The coke and chips are

216

heavenly, Om mani padmi hum, the Sadza is so filling, hiha, hiha, hiha. Wisdom must come with food.

If you have enjoyed *Finding A WayHome* consider these other fine books in **Mmap Fiction and Drama Series** from *Mwanaka Media and Publishing*:

The Water Cycle by Andrew Nyongesa
A Conversation…, A Contact by Tendai Rinos Mwanaka
A Dark Energy by Tendai Rinos Mwanaka
Keys in the River: New and Collected Stories by Tendai Rinos Mwanaka
How The Twins Grew Up/Makurire Akaita Mapatya by Milutin Djurickovic and Tendai Rinos Mwanaka
White Man Walking by John Eppel
The Big Noise and Other Noises by Christopher Kudyahakudadirwe
Tiny Human Protection Agency by Megan Landman
Ashes by Ken Weene and Umar O. Abdul
Notes From A Modern Chimurenga: Collected Struggle Stories by Tendai Rinos Mwanaka
Another Chance by Chinweike Ofodile
Pano Chalo/Frawn of the Great by Stephen Mpashi, translated by Austin Kaluba
Kumafulatsi by Wonder Guchu
The Policeman Also Dies and Other Plays by Solomon A. Awuzie
Fragmented Lives by Imali J Abala
In the Beyond by Talent Madhuku
Zororo Risina Zororo by Oscar Gwiriri
Sword of Vengeance by Olatubosun David

Soon to be released

Thorn in Flesh by Phillip Marufu
Conversation with my Mother by Wonder Guchu

https://facebook.com/MwanakaMediaAndPublishing/

Printed in the United States
by Baker & Taylor Publisher Services